BEATING
Bully O'Brien

Although born in Wisconsin, KAREN MUELLER COOMBS grew up in the Northern Alberta town of Grande Prairie. The first bully she encountered was in her first grade classroom. Karen didn't do anything when the bully picked on her. Then one day he started picking on her best friend. That did it. Karen gave him a black eye. He didn't bully Karen or her friends after that. Many years later, the awful way he had made her feel helped Karen write about those feelings in *Beating Bully O'Brien*.

Today Karen lives with her husband Jon, her son, Cameron, and her daughter, Carlin, in Carlsbad, California. Now that her children are older, they have run into a few bullies themselves. So far Cameron and Carlin haven't blackened any eyes. Karen hopes they won't have to.

BEATING
Bully O'Brien

KAREN MUELLER COOMBS

AN AVON CAMELOT BOOK

BEATING BULLY O'BRIEN is an original publication of Avon Books. This work
has never before appeared in book form.

AVON BOOKS
A division of
The Hearst Corporation
1350 Avenue of the Americas
New York, New York 10019

Copyright © 1991 by Karen Mueller Coombs
Published by arrangement with the author
Library of Congress Catalog Card Number: 90-93200
ISBN: 0-380-75935-7
RL: 4.6

First Avon Camelot Printing: January 1991

Printed in the U.S.A.

OPM   10   9   8   7   6   5   4   3

For Cameron, my very special son,
and
for Carlin, my very special daughter.
With love.
XXOXXOXXO

Chapter One

"Here's a good-bye gift." Tink drew back a fist and slugged Rocky right in the mouth.

Salty blood oozed onto Rocky's tongue. Salty tears stung his eyes. He didn't let them spill. Instead, he did what he usually did. He joked. "Right in the kisser," he spluttered, hurrying down the street. "Right in the *kisser*. And I haven't even used it yet."

"Haven't used what yet?" asked Daniel, catching up and handing Rocky a dirty gym sock to wipe his mouth.

"My kisser," said Rocky. "I mean I haven't used my kisser as a kisser yet."

"Give it time," said Daniel. "You're only ten."

"At this rate, I might not see eleven!" joked Rocky. Joking helped him ignore the lump stuck in the back of his throat. He swallowed, then took a deep, slow breath, glad Tink had a weak punch. In spite of the blood, it was his pride, not his lip, that hurt.

Rocky gave Daniel back his sock. "Well, I'm glad that's out of the way—until tomorrow." Rocky cupped his hands around his mouth and shouted, "JOIN US TOMORROW AT THE SAME TIME, SAME PLACE, TO ONCE

1

AGAIN SEE TINK O'BRIEN MASH ROCKY RYAN INTO MUSH.''

Daniel shook a clenched fist under Rocky's chin. ''One good clop in the chops might end it.''

''I can't,'' Rocky hissed. ''What if I sprain my wrist or bust a finger?''

''Then I get to draw nasty pictures on your cast.''

''The only nasty picture you'll see is my mother stuffing me in my viola case for missing my competition next week. *That's* what will happen if I break a finger.''

''But you can't let Tink O'Brien pound on you every day for the rest of the year. It's only March. One lucky sock in the eye and you won't be able to see your viola to play it!''

Rocky stomped a paper cup lying on the sidewalk. ''That's what I'd like to do to Tink O'Brien,'' he muttered, but it was only for Daniel's benefit.

''Man, you really tick me off,'' said Daniel. ''You talk about what you'd *like* to do, but you never do anything. You're acting like a wimp.''

Rocky shivered, even though the spring sun was warm. ''What I'd like to know is, do I *look* like a wimp? Is that why Tink picked *me* out to punch?''

''Who knows why Tink picked you?'' answered Daniel. ''What difference does it make anyway? Maybe you let a door slam in Tink's face last week. Maybe Tink doesn't like your chin. The reason doesn't matter. What matters is, what are you going to do about it?'' Daniel put his hands on his hips, scrunched his eyebrows and lowered his head at Rocky. ''You *have* to do something.''

''You're right,'' Rocky agreed. ''Viola or no viola, I have to do something. But what? Even if I *don't* wreck myself fighting Tink, I'll end up dog meat. Tink has a brother in junior high who's supposed to be the size of a refrigerator.''

2

"Yeah," said Daniel. "And if I hear that threat one more time I'm going to puke."

"You mean this threat?" Rocky cupped his hands again and shouted in Daniel's ear, "MY BROTHER'S A BOXER AND IF YOU LAY A FINGER ON ME HE'S GOING TO COME AND MUSH YOUR BRAINS!"

Daniel bent over and gagged into his gym bag.

Rocky laughed. With a friend like Daniel, he couldn't stay gloomy for long. But if he wanted to keep Daniel as his friend, he had to get Tink O'Brien off his case. No one wanted to hang out with a kid who let himself get pushed around.

Besides, he was tired of walking around with his head down, afraid of what—or who—he might see. He was tired of wincing whenever someone made a fist, twitching when someone yelled, leaping out of his shorts when a book dropped. He was tired of feeling like he might burst into tears at the silliest times for no reason at all. Clowning around helped a bit, but he always had a knot of fear in his gut.

"Hey," said Daniel, "there's no law that says you have to just stand around and get socked, is there?"

"You mean you want me to play chicken and run?"

Daniel shrugged. "Why not?"

Rocky shook his head. "That would be a *real* wimpy thing to do. Then I'd have to listen to Tink clucking at me for the rest of the year." He stopped to feel his swollen lip. "If I was getting picked on by anyone else, I think I would cut out. If I ran from Tink, I'd never live it down."

"I see what you mean," agreed Daniel. "No one would cluck if they saw you running away from Tink's big blob of a brother."

"Hey!" said Rocky, slapping his forehead. "That just gave me an idea. I don't know why I didn't think of it

3

before. Sure, Tink has a big blob of a brother. But I've got a big sister! What good is a big sister if she can't, just this once, help out her precious baby brother?"

"What good will it do to get Paula to beat up Tink's brother?" Daniel asked, his glasses bobbing as he wrinkled his nose.

"Not Tink's brother, maggot breath. I'm going to get Paula to beat up Tink."

"You're joking! You've been letting some new kid at school make hamburger out of you every day for the last week and you haven't done a single thing about it?" Paula rolled her eyes upward.

Rocky and Paula were standing in the kitchen. Paula had just gobbled four cookies in a record thirty seconds. Brown crumbs were strung across her bottom lip and she flicked her tongue at them while she stared at Rocky.

"Man has to learn to overcome violence without resorting to violence," Rocky explained.

Paula smacked her forehead with her palm. "Who said that? Ferdinand the bull?"

The Story of Ferdinand had always been Rocky's favorite book. Like the bull, Rocky preferred flowers to fighting.

"No, Ferdinand didn't say it. Martin Luther King, Jr., said it. Something like it anyway. Ferdinand would agree with him though."

"So how'd you learn about Martin Luther King, Jr.?" Paula asked.

"We studied him in January for Martin Luther King, Jr., Day, of course," Rocky explained. "Where were *you?* And then we were supposed to read a book for Black History Month, so I read a biography about him. He had some interesting stuff to say about using nonviolence instead of violence."

"Jeez," said Paula in a disgusted voice. "You've gone soft."

"Not soft," said Rocky. "Peaceable. But don't tell Dad, eh?" he added. "You know what he'd say."

"Do I!" said Paula. She put a hand on her hip and shook one finger of the other at Rocky in an imitation of their father. "I'm disappointed in you, son. A *man* has to stand up for *himself* in this life. Don't—(shake)—you—(shake)—ever—(shake)—forget—(shake)—that."

"How could I forget?" groaned Rocky. "I hear it every day. It's just that Dad's idea of standing up for myself is different from my idea.

"Anyway, is a ten year old considered a man?" he added, hoping Paula would say no, but sort of hoping Paula would say yes.

Paula furrowed her brow. "That depends on the ten year old. *I* would have been a man at ten—if I hadn't been a female. But you?" She wriggled her fingers under Rocky's nose. "You play the *vee-o-la!*"

Rocky sneered at his fourteen-year-old sister and poked her in the arm. "Yeah," he taunted, "but when you were ten you were also *one hundred and fifty pounds* of *flab!*"

Paula locked one arm around Rocky's head and gave his scalp a light knuckle rub with her free hand. "You can just forget about my help after a remark like that," she snarled.

"I'm sorry," squeaked Rocky. He'd only told the truth, but the truth wasn't always something a person wanted to hear—like Daniel calling him a wimp. And take a few other truths about himself for instance. (Was he *really* a wimp?) Although he had fantasies about being Han Solo, he was as ordinary as straight brown hair, hazel eyes, size six feet, two cowlicks and three warts could make him.

Even his brain was ordinary. Seldom did he get an *A.* Never did he get a *D.* Ordinary.

5

In fact, if it weren't for his musical talent, he thought, he'd be downright boring. And that was the truth.

So why, he wondered, had Tink O'Brien picked him out to bully? He was no more conspicuous than a single ant in an anthill.

At last Paula let go of Rocky's head.

"Please don't be ticked," Rocky pleaded, rubbing his scalp. "I really need your help." To his disgust, his voice cracked. He cleared his throat, pretending he had a frog in it.

"You want me to meet you at the entrance to our cul-de-sac after school tomorrow and beat the snot out of this Tink O'Brien for you. That it?"

"Yeah, that's it. I don't think it'll take much. One punch should do it. From you, maybe even a loud warning."

"How will I recognize this Tink?"

"Simple. Dark hair, clenched fists, nasty sneer. If you're still in doubt, just look for the kid pounding the stuffing out of me."

"Sounds easy enough. What's the catch?"

"No catch."

"Then why don't you do it yourself?"

Rocky held up his hands and wriggled his fingers under Paula's nose. "Because I play the vee-o-la."

"I thought it was because you were peaceable," sneered Paula.

"Yeah, that too," said Rocky.

"Well, I don't think getting me to do your fighting for you was exactly what Martin Luther King had in mind."

Rocky thought about that for a minute. "I'm new at this nonviolence stuff," he answered finally. "I think getting you to help would be okay this once. And like I said, maybe even a loud warning will be enough."

"Okay," said Paula. "I'll do it—"

"Gee, thank—" Rocky began.

"—for five bucks," Paula finished.

"Five bucks?" Rocky squealed. "That's two weeks' allowance!"

"Your choice, kid." Paula turned to go.

Rocky thought fast. Was it worth two weeks' allowance to get Tink O'Brien to quit bashing him? No—it was worth *four* weeks' allowance. He was getting off easy.

"You got it," he told Paula. "But you *don't* get it unless you do the job right. That means no bucks until one entire school week goes by without one jab in the jaw."

Paula's shoulders bobbed. She reached for another cookie. "It's a deal."

"So when will you do it?" asked Rocky.

"When I do it."

Rocky knew he wouldn't get any more of an answer than that out of Paula. He got out his viola. "You better watch out, Tink O'Brien," he said to the air as he plucked at the strings. " 'Cuz this is what my big sister's gonna do to your eyelashes."

And for the first time in days, his heart was quiet.

Chapter Two

Rocky and Daniel dawdled after school the next day, making certain Tink had plenty of time to reach Ambush Corner, the corner Rocky *had* to use to get home because the Ryans lived at the end of a dead-end street. Rocky had tried cutting through yards and over fences to avoid the corner, but Mrs. Bonner had threatened to have him arrested for trespassing if he didn't quit climbing her fence, and Mr. Tachuk's dog acted as though he'd rip out Rocky's throat whenever Rocky tried to come into the yard. So he had no choice but to go past Ambush Corner.

"Let's go," he told Daniel at last. "If Paula's coming today, she should be there by now." He leaped into the air, threw a punch skyward. "Jeez, what a relief! No fat lip today. Or tomorrow. Or the day after. *Thank you, Paula!*"

"Maybe you better hold off on your *merci*'s until after Paula's done her duty," warned Daniel. Daniel always sprinkled French words into his conversations. His family, the Tuans, was from Vietnam and spoke French as well as English and Vietnamese.

"She'll do it," Rocky said confidently, rubbing his thumb and two fingers together. "No clash, no cash."

8

Daniel dug around in his backpack and pulled out a wadded-up woolen scarf. "You're lucky I never empty my bag. Now we have this—just in case."

"Just in case what?"

"Just in case you need another blood blotter."

"Won't need it," said Rocky as they neared the corner. "Paula's already there. And so is Tink."

Paula was sitting on a bus bench practically next to Tink, who was leaning against a maple tree. Paula's arms were spread out on the back of the bench and she was looking around as though trying to guess which of the kids walking home was Tink.

When the boys got close to the corner, Rocky slowed to a saunter, giving Tink plenty of opportunity to attack.

"I've got another present for you," Tink taunted.

"Where'll it be delivered today?" Rocky asked. He could really joke now that salvation was near. "The chin? The eye? The mouth? Better yet, why don't you just deliver it to my bodyguard?"

He looked at Paula to see what she was doing. Nothing! Paula was doing nothing!

Rocky narrowed his eyes at Paula and jerked his head in Tink's direction, in case Paula hadn't figured out which kid to bash.

Paula heaved herself off the bench. Rocky grinned with relief. But Paula only sneered at him before she spit a wad of gum into the gutter, spun around and stalked off.

"Uh, oh," said Daniel.

"That's your *bodyguard?"* Tink asked sarcastically.

"You got it," sighed Rocky, his mouth suddenly as dry as feathers. He braced himself for Tink's punch, then held out his hand for Daniel's wadded-up woolen scarf.

* * *

It was supper time. Paula had just come home, so Rocky hadn't had a chance to yell at her about desertion and other mean tricks. All he could do as the four Ryans sat down at the table was curl back his upper lip and lower his eyebrows at his sister.

Paula put her thumb on her nose and waggled her fingers in Rocky's direction.

"What's this?" asked their mother. "You two having a tiff?"

Actually it's more like the Civil War, thought Rocky. Gray against blue. Paula gets to be gray. I get to be blue—bruise blue. But there's no way I'm going to tell what's going on, because Dad will be ticked at me for not standing up for myself. I just hope Paula doesn't blab.

Rocky could imagine the scene if she did:

"Haven't I told you to stand up for yourself?" Mr. Ryan would ask quietly. Then he would hold up his fists, which looked like small tree stumps, and say, "What do you think these things are for?"

"They're for playing the viola," Mrs. Ryan would say. With luck, that would be the end of it.

"Your lip is swollen," Rocky's mother said then, bringing Rocky back to the present.

"I played Keep Away at recess again," Rocky said quickly. It wasn't really a fib. He had played Keep Away.

"That game has been causing you a lot of fat lips this past week," his mother said. "You be careful. The competition is next week. You want to win that scholarship to music camp, don't you?"

Rocky nodded.

His father sighed.

Rocky knew all this talk about swollen lips and music would encourage Paula to blab. And he knew he couldn't give her a chance to do that. So he decided to talk constantly and not let her say one word during the entire meal.

"Mrs. Crayton gave us tons of math homework today," he started. "And during recess this morning Cindy Fedova fell on the concrete and ripped all the skin off her knees. We heard her screeching way over on the other side of the school yard. And then . . ."

It worked. Paula kept her mouth shut except to shovel food into it. Even his parents didn't say a word until they'd cleaned their plates.

"Give it a rest," said Mr. Ryan then.

"Give what a rest?" asked Rocky.

"Your tongue. My ears," explained Mr. Ryan, tugging at his beard. "I swear, I never heard a kid yap so much. Look at your plate. You've been talking so much, you haven't even had time to chew."

"Ah, I'm not . . . really . . . hungry," fibbed Rocky, just as his stomach rumbled loud enough to rattle his eyeballs.

"Why don't you get the dessert out of the fridge for me then?" suggested Rocky's mother.

Rocky carried the bowl of raspberry Jell-O carefully, because Mrs. Ryan made dessert when she got home from work. That meant Jell-O never had time to set, even when she used the quick-set method. It was always as thick as a milkshake and slithered around the bowl. Since it was a pain to eat with a spoon, Rocky usually drank his.

Rocky was nearly to the table when Paula asked, "You know what brother twit asked me to do for him?"

Oh, no! thought Rocky. If she rats, I'm dead. He stood frozen behind Paula's chair, wondering what to do. He knew it was no use telling Paula to shut up. If Paula wanted to blab, she'd blab.

11

Mr. and Mrs. Ryan waited, their eyebrows raised at Paula.

Rocky did the only thing he could—and his aim was perfect.

"Aaarrrrgh!" shrieked Paula as cold, watery Jell-O sloshed down her back and over her shoulder. She leaped to her feet to tackle Rocky. She snagged him by the T-shirt, and Rocky *knew* he'd never live to see eleven. But then Paula slipped in some Jell-O and landed right on her butt next to the table.

"Oh, no, you don't," said Mrs. Ryan when Paula, growling under her breath, started after Rocky again. "No way do you slop Jell-O all over this house. Strip right there." Then she pointed a finger at Rocky and his father. "You two, out!"

"Still tripping over your feet, eh?" asked Mr. Ryan as they made a hasty exit.

Rocky nodded, certain he was going to get a lecture about his coordination. But his father just sighed and said, "Maybe it's only a stage—like nonstop talking." Then he grabbed the newspaper and headed for his favorite chair, sucking a splatter of Jell-O off his sleeve as he went.

Rocky sighed. More than anything he wanted to please his father. But his father wanted a son who was good at sports, who could slam dunk a basketball, blitz a quarterback and smack a homer out of center field. What he had was a son who played the viola. He also had a son who didn't want to fight. But Mr. Ryan didn't know that. And he wouldn't know it if Rocky had anything to say about it.

Rocky heard Paula stomp into the bathroom. The shower hissed.

"Okay, Rocky. Your turn. Come in here and clean this up," his mother called.

By now, the Jell-O was even runnier, but Rocky figured out he could scrape it into one glob with the rubber edge of the dustpan, then push it onto the pan with a rubber scraper and dump it down the sink. It took him a good quarter hour just to do that much, but it was worth every second. He even hummed "Whistle While You Work" as he scraped and scooped. He was scrubbing Jell-O stains off the floor when he heard his mother, who was putting dishes away, make a strange gulping noise.

"Gee, Mom," Rocky said, getting to his feet, a sick feeling squirming through his gut at the thought of his mother in tears, "I'm really sorry if I upset you. I didn't mean—"

"Oh-ho-ho!" shrieked Mrs. Ryan then. "Whoo-hoo-hoo!" She leaned over the sink, her shoulders shaking.

Rocky's jaw fell practically to his high-tops. "What's so funny?" he asked.

"I never . . . I never . . . never saw . . . anything so funny . . . as the look on Paula's face . . . when she got that lapful of Jell-O," said Mrs. Ryan between giggles. "And then, when she was sitting on the floor . . . in the middle of . . . all that red glop. Oh, hoo-hoo-hoo!"

"Why all the hysterics?" asked Mr. Ryan, coming into the kitchen.

"Mom was just remembering the look on Paula's face when I *accidentally* spilled the Jell-O on her," explained Rocky.

Mr. Ryan tugged at his beard, smoothed his mustache and grinned. "It *was* kinda funny," he said. "Which reminds me. I forgot to thank you." He put his arm around Rocky and gave him a squeeze.

"What for?"

Rocky's dad chuckled. "For *not* dumping that slop on

me." He laughed again, swatted his wife on the bottom and went back to his newspaper.

"Oh, mush!" said Rocky, as he resumed his scrubbing.

His mother only chuckled and said, "Oh, mush yourself."

Chapter Three

Later, Rocky was lying on his bed eating peanut butter crackers and multiplying two thousand three hundred fifty-nine by forty-six when Paula barged into his room.

"I ought to rip out your tonsils," she snarled, planting one knee in the middle of Rocky's back and shoving his face into the bed.

Whenever Paula tackled him, Rocky tried to think of something else. This time, since his nose was crammed into the bed, he thought about his Anchors Aweigh bedspread. He took a good whiff. Sweaty sneakers, he thought. The bedspread smells just like sweaty sneakers.

After another whiff, Rocky squirmed out from under Paula's knee and sat up. "I'd rather have a *doctor* rip out my tonsils, if you don't mind," he said. "And anyway, I'm the one who should be ripping out tonsils. What good is a big sister who won't stand up for her little brother—even when she's being *paid* to do it?"

"What good is a boy who won't stand up for himself?" Paula snapped.

"I *was* standing up for myself—in a way," Rocky began. "I just used my head instead of my fists is all. Getting you

15

to help would get Tink off my back and save my hands for the competition at the same time. That's what I figured.''

"Yeah, but when you asked for help you left out one little detail,'' Paula sneered. "One teensy-weensy detail.''

"What detail? I told you everything!''

"Everything except . . .'' Paula paused as though she were a storybook detective about to name the murderer.

"Except *what?*'' Rocky shouted. "Except what?''

"Except the fact that Tink O'Brien is a *girl!*'' The word "girl'' dripped off Paula's tongue like slug slime.

Rocky scrinched his nose in puzzlement. "What difference does that make?'' he asked.

For one second Paula said nothing. "What difference does *that* make?'' she squeaked, bugging out her eyes in disbelief. "What difference does that make? You might as well ask me to dissect Kermit the Frog as ask me to beat on some skinny girl with ponytails.''

"She's bigger than me,'' said Rocky loudly.

"Yeah, she's got a coupla inches on you,'' Paula agreed, "but jeez, a girl's a girl.''

"*You're* a great one to be telling me *that!*'' squealed Rocky. "Next you'll be telling me all girls are soft and pink and helpless—like you. Well, you know what I say to that? I say HA!''

"And you know what I say to you?'' hissed Paula. "I say you better start standing up for yourself.''

"And you know what I say *back* to you?'' Rocky yelled. "I say you sound just like Dad. And you're not Dad, so you can't tell me what to do!''

Paula ran her fingers through her short, damp curls, then plunked down beside Rocky on the bed. "You know,'' she said, "you're right. I do sound like Dad.''

"Yeah, you sound real mawko.''

"Mawko?''

16

"You know. Tough, he-man stuff."

Paula laughed. "I think you mean *macho.*" Only she pronounced it *maw-cho.*

"Whatever," said Rocky. "Anyway, I get enough of that stuff from him without you starting on me too."

"Yeah, I guess you do," agreed Paula.

Rocky narrowed his eyes at his sister. "You all right?" he asked.

"As all right as anyone drowned in Jell-O should feel. Why?"

" 'Cuz I think you just agreed with me about something." Rocky tongued the tip of his finger and touched it to the wall as though to mark a special occasion.

"Real cute," said Paula, giving him a shove on the shoulder and toppling him over. "Just because we argue a lot doesn't mean I don't care what happens to you. And just because I didn't pound that kid today, doesn't mean I want you to keep getting beaten on." She flopped backwards, her hands behind her head. "So what are you going to do?"

Rocky shrugged. "I guess I'll have to wait until after the competition," he said, "and then bop her a good one myself, Martin Luther King or no Martin Luther King, Ferdinand or no Ferdinand."

"Wrong." Paula shook her head. "If Dad ever found out you hit a girl he'd string you up by your toenails. You'll have to think of something else."

"Terrific!" said Rocky. "I've got to get Tink to quit pounding me, only I can't have any help and I can't hit her myself, even if I believed in hitting people, which I don't."

"You got it," said Paula. She flicked her finger against Rocky's forehead. "Good luck, fiddle fingers." She pushed herself off the bed and clumped out of the room.

17

I need more than luck, thought Rocky, when Paula had slammed the door behind her, I need a miracle.

The next morning when Rocky was brushing his teeth, he got his miracle. His toothpaste was making him foam at the mouth, just like Disney's dog, Old Yeller. Rabies! he thought. I'll tell Mom I have rabies and can't go to school. Then he shook his head. Naw, his mom would never fall for that. But thinking about rabies had given him an idea. He ran steaming hot water over a washcloth and held it to his face. "One fake fever coming up," he muttered.

"Now if your fever gets any worse, or you need me for anything, call me," Rocky's mother reminded him before she left for work. "Here's a bucket in case you need to throw up. And if you start feeling hungry, there's soup in the cupboard." She kissed Rocky on the forehead. "See, that aspirin went right to work," she said. "You feel cooler already."

Rocky managed a weak wave as his mother went out the door. I suppose I should feel guilty for lying about being sick, he thought. But I don't. One little fib is better than being terrorized.

Rocky spent part of the morning watching the game shows *Stump the Champ* and *Sore Losers* on TV. After *Sore Losers* he rummaged in the fridge and found some leftover lasagna. He mixed himself a bubble gum ice cream milk shake, grabbed a handful of coconut cookies and got out his viola. He arranged the food around his chair, placing it carefully so he could munch and slurp without dropping crumbs or blobs in the viola. Then he looked around him, sighed a contented sigh and started to practice his piece for the competition.

18

Suddenly his mother was standing beside him, her mouth pulled to one side, her brows lowered.

"F-e-e-e-e-ling better?" she asked.

Rocky's face scrunched, his tongue flipped and a piece of bubble gum caught in his throat. "Uuuh—yeah," he said after he'd stopped gagging. "A lot better. But why are you home now?" His mother usually didn't get home from the flower shop where she worked until nearly six.

"I thought I'd better check on you," she explained. She felt Rocky's forehead, studied his lunch, then sighed. "I suspected as much." She took the viola and set it aside, then led Rocky over to the sofa and pulled him down beside her.

"Okay, out with it," she ordered.

"Out with what?"

"With whatever has you so upset you'd rather play sick than go to school."

Rocky thought what would happen if he told his mother about Tink. Her help might cause more problems for him than he already had, he decided, which was what usually happened when parents tried to help.

First she'd phone his principal, Barfbag Bailey.

"Does this bullying occur on school property?" Barfbag would ask. Since Tink had never done anything to Rocky at school, Barfbag would say, "I'm sorry, there's nothing I can do about events that occur off school grounds. Perhaps you should call the other child's parents."

If his mother did that, and Tink ratted to the class, Rocky was doomed to be laughed out of the fifth grade.

"Know what?" he could imagine tattletale Christina Tate shouting all over the school, "Rocky had to get his *mommy* to phone Tink's *mommy* to get her to stop beating him up." Even if he won he lost.

And his mother would lose too, if his father found out

19

she had helped Rocky. "You're turning that boy into a sissy!" he would accuse her. "Let him fight his own battles."

No, it was best to say nothing.

"I'm not upset," he fibbed to his mother. "I really was feeling sick this morning."

His mother studied him, her eyes narrowed. She reached out and gently touched his lip, the one he had split the day before, when Tink punched him. "Okay, if that's the way you want it," she told him. "But you're going to school tomorrow."

Rocky nodded agreement.

"Just one thing," his mother added. "You can tell your father or me anything."

Rocky nodded.

"Anything," she repeated.

"I know, Mom," said Rocky quietly, almost believing, but knowing it wasn't quite true.

As his mother drove away, Rocky wondered if he had been wrong not to tell her about Tink. No, he decided. If he told his mother, either it would be World War III in the Ryan household or he wouldn't be able to go back to school without wearing a disguise.

A disguise!

Of course! thought Rocky. Why didn't I think of that before!

Chapter Four

Mrs. Crayton was going to make an announcement. Rocky knew she had something to report because, first, as usual, she stood up and tugged at the warty pink sweater she wore every single day of the school year. Today's announcement was one Rocky would have preferred not to hear.

"Listen up," said Mrs. Crayton, tapping her ruler on her desk. "After lunch we're getting a new student in the room. She's moving over from Mr. Shopik's class, so some of you might know her. Even so, try to make her feel welcome."

"Who is it?" asked Tim Mathews. He was probably hoping Michelle Taylor was moving in. The whole fifth grade knew Tim had a crush on Michelle. Every time she said hello to him he blushed and punched the closest kid. No one stood near Tim when Michelle was around.

"Catherine O'Brien," said Mrs. Crayton.

The name didn't sink into Rocky's brain for a second. Then he got a jolt, the kind you'd get if your raft had been floating peacefully on a pond and then suddenly whooshed over a waterfall. He reached across the aisle and up a seat

21

to jab Daniel. "Is that who I think it is?" he whispered. "Tell me it isn't."

Daniel bobbed his shoulders. "I think," he answered, "Catherine O'Brien must be *le nom* of the dreaded Tink O'Brien." He reached back and put a hand on Rocky's arm. "Might I interest you in some life insurance?" he asked.

Rocky peered sideways at the white leather sneakers planted beside his desk.

"Can I borrow your eraser?" a voice somewhere above the sneakers asked.

Rocky forced himself to look up. He crossed his eyes slightly so the face above him would be a blur. He forced his lips into a sort of smile. But he didn't really feel like smiling. He felt like throwing up.

He was going to say, "Sure," but he was afraid it would come out a squeak, so he just nodded at the blur. The blur blinked, grabbed the eraser off his desk and disappeared down the aisle.

Rocky shut his eyes, took a gulp of air to calm his jitters. That was the closest he'd ever been to Tink without getting socked. We've been in the same room for sixty-two minutes, thirty-five seconds, and I'm still in one piece, he thought. She hasn't so much as pinched me. I wonder what she's waiting for?

"Borrow your colored pencils?"

Rocky jerked. His eyes flew open and he looked right at Tink, forgetting to make his gaze fuzzy. She was grinning. It was an ordinary grin, but to Rocky it looked like the wolf's leer in "Little Red Riding Hood." Except Tink has a space between her front teeth you could spit a raisin through, he told himself. But then, how do I know the wolf didn't have a space between his teeth too? Maybe all bullies have spaces between their front teeth.

I doubt the wolf had jumpy eyes, he thought, noticing that Tink's eyes never settled on anything. Her eyes flit all over the place. They sure are big though. And the same blue as those flowers Mom planted.

The flowers were violas. Mrs. Ryan had planted them for Rocky because they were spelled the same as Rocky's instrument. Rocky always forgot and called them *vee-olas,* like his instrument, instead of *vi-ola,* which was the name of the flower.

Anyway, Tink's eyes certainly are the same pretty blue as those flowers, he thought.

Rocky clapped a hand over his mouth, even though he hadn't said anything out loud. I can't believe I even *thought* that, he told himself. That's like saying a rattlesnake has pretty teeth. Sheesh!

He reached into his desk and grabbed his colored pencils. He thrust them at Tink, hoping she wouldn't notice his hand shaking.

"Thanks," she said, and spun around and went back to her desk, one of her long, dark ponytails flinging out from her head and twitching him across the cheek as she turned.

Daniel looked over his shoulder at Rocky and raised his eyebrows. Rocky shrugged.

"Just look at this, will you?" Rocky asked Daniel later, after the dismissal bell rang. "Just look at this!" He held out his eraser and his colored pencils. "Good old Rocky thought he'd practice the Golden Rule. You know, treat others the way you want to be treated. So what do I get in return? An eraser poked full of pencil holes and a pack of pencils that look like they've been attacked by woodpeckers. You know what this means, don't you?"

"That she's mad at your eraser and pencils?" asked Daniel.

"No, zit head. Don't you see? It's a warning of what she's going to do to me."

"Chew on you and poke holes in you," commented Daniel. "That I'll have to see."

"You can joke because you're not the one she picks on," said Rocky.

"Well, you were in the same room all afternoon and nothing happened."

"I figure she's too smart to do anything at school where Mrs. Crayton could catch her. As usual, she's waiting till after. Only this time I'm going to be ready for her. This time I'm going to outsmart her."

"What are you going to do, *mon ami?* Sprout wings and fly home?" asked Daniel.

"You'll see," Rocky replied, removing a lumpy paper bag from his desk. "But first I have to stop in the washroom."

"Yipes!" squealed Daniel a few minutes later, when Rocky came out of the washroom. "I didn't recognize you. I thought some creepy girl had sneaked in there to have a peek."

"So, how do I look?"

Daniel studied his friend. Rocky had hair that fell to his shoulders in long, dark waves. A pair of yellow cat's eye sunglasses perched on his nose and he was wearing a pink nylon jacket that hung nearly to the knees of his jeans. "Weird," said Daniel. "You look weird."

"Think I'll pass?"

"Yeah, you'll pass—for Miss Piggy's sister," Daniel said. "What gives?"

"I figured this way I look like a junior high girl and I might be able to sneak past Tink without her recognizing me."

"Might work," said Daniel. "The lipstick's a nice touch.

You smeared it a bit right there though," he said, jabbing a finger at Rocky's bottom lip.

"I haven't had much practice with lipstick," Rocky hissed. "Anyway, it's worth a try. Now what do you think? Will she recognize me?"

"There is one thing she'll recognize," Daniel said. "Unless you get rid of it, you might as well prepare to get slugged."

"What? Get rid of what?"

"Me," said Daniel. "Don't you think Tink will wonder why I've suddenly started walking home with a girl who looks like leftover pizza?"

"You're right," said Rocky, smacking his forehead. "You go on ahead. I'll catch up after I'm safely past Ambush Corner." He tugged at a hank of hair that trailed across his nose.

Daniel shook his head. "No way," he said. *"You* go first. I'll come behind. If you think I'm going to miss this performance, you're crazier than you look."

Chapter Five

As he got closer to Ambush Corner, Rocky took shorter steps and swung his rear from side to side, thinking he would look more like a girl that way. Behind him Daniel sniggered, then shrilled out a loud wolf whistle.

Rocky turned and scowled. A lot of help Daniel was.

Rocky quit his hip waggling, dug three purple bubble gum balls out of his pocket, popped them into his mouth and started to chew. His stomach felt the way it did when he waited for his music exams to start, as if a fiery volcano was rumbling inside it, drying up all his spit. Chewing gum usually helped.

Today Tink was sitting on the bus bench next to the maple tree. She stared right at Rocky as he came toward her. The harder she stared, the harder he chewed.

Rocky's leg muscles twitched, begging to break into a gallop, but he forced himself to stroll along like he hadn't a worry.

I'm not dressed any weirder than a lot of kids, he told himself, so it's not my outfit she's staring at. Maybe something else is giving me away. But he couldn't think what it might be.

Daniel! he thought, but when he spun around to look, his friend was a half block away, pretending to study some nasty pictures sprayed on a fence.

Rocky strolled. Tink stared. Closer and closer he got to the bench. His volcano was really rumbling now, and he could feel a fiery flush creep up his neck, just like red-hot lava creeping toward the mouth of a real volcano. Cripes! he thought. If I blush she'll know me for sure. What can I do?

The harder he thought, the harder he chomped. His scissoring jaws must have put his brain in motion, because he got an idea. The sunglasses already covered the top part of his face. If Tink couldn't see the bottom part either, for sure she couldn't recognize him. What he needed was for his volcano to erupt—sort of.

Rocky took a ragged, deep breath, smoothed the bubble gum over his tongue and started to blow. The bubble was soon over his mouth. Rocky blew. Tink stared.

He was nearly at the bench. The bubble was over his nose. Rocky blew. Tink stared.

He was beside the bench. The bubble was up to his cat's eye sunglasses. Rocky blew. Tink stared. The bubble—blew.

"A-a-a-agh!" Rocky dropped his book bag and started clawing at the gum. If there was anything he hated, it was having his nose covered. It reminded him of the times Paula shoved his face into his bed and made him feel as though he were going to smother.

"Yuck!" he croaked, pulling at a strand of goo clinging to his lip and chin. "Ah, double yuck!" He grabbed a string that went from his nose to his glasses. And that's when he made his mistake.

Right next to that string was a long thick curl that had strayed over his brow and was now pinched in the hinge of his glasses. When Rocky grabbed and jerked, the string of gum came loose. So did his sunglasses. So did his wig.

Rocky stood, one hand holding a string of gum, one hand keeping the crooked wig on his head. He watched Tink get off the bench and take two steps toward him.

She looks like a vulture who's just found a carcass, he thought mournfully, feeling rooted to the sidewalk like a deer frozen in a car's headlights.

Now Tink was practically nose to nose with him. He waited, certain her blue eyes were burning holes in him, just like in a horror book he had read, certain her teeth were growing into fangs that would sink into his jugular, certain her swinging ponytails were coiling into hissing snakes that would wrap around his windpipe and strangle him.

"Ferdinand, Ferdinand, Ferdinand," Rocky chanted to himself, willing himself not to fling his arms over his face and neck. He forced a smile through the purple goo. "Care for some gum?" he asked in a tiny voice.

For a second Tink looked confused. Her forehead furrowed, her eyebrows lowered and she started to chew on one corner of her bottom lip.

"Got any without lipstick and spit?" she asked.

"Sorry." Rocky shrugged. "What you see is what you get," he added, hoping humor would distract Tink from her usual path. But it was no go.

Tink raised a fist. "And this is what you get," she said.

Rocky considered covering his face after all, but decided not to. What if she landed a lucky blow and broke his finger? He also thought about running, but that would be a *real* chicken thing to do, and he'd already decided he didn't want people clucking at him for the rest of his life.

Then Tink hesitated and Rocky thought there was hope. Perhaps Tink didn't want to hurt her hand either. But she only looked at his face, said, "Who wants to touch that goop?"—and slammed Rocky right in the gut.

It wasn't a hard punch, but Rocky hadn't been expecting a belly blow, so it knocked the breath out of him. He bent double and made short gasping sounds like a pig with the hiccups.

The wig and sunglasses fell to the sidewalk. Even while he gulped for air, Rocky thought, Please don't let me cry. And please don't let my dad drive by.

Daniel raced up. "You okay?" he said. He held out a piece of plastic wrap smeared with chocolate frosting and said, "It's all I could find."

"I—don't—think—I'll—need—it," gasped Rocky. "No—blood." His breath was coming back now and he straightened up.

He was surprised to see Tink still hanging around, though nearly out of earshot. He shook his fist in her direction, but she only grinned and stuck out her tongue.

"You want me to bash her?" asked Daniel. "I'll do it for you. I will."

"Maybe," Rocky answered. Then he looked at Tink again and shook his head. "Naw. Remember. I . . . told you . . . my dad . . . says I have to learn to . . . stand up for myself. But he also says . . . never hit a girl."

"Pardonez-moi," said Daniel. "I forgot. Boy, that makes it tough. You really are caught between a cliff and a buffalo stampede. Ha-ha!"

"Yeah, ha-ha," said Rocky.

"So, what *are* you going to do?" Daniel asked.

Rocky shrugged. "You tell me."

Daniel started licking the chocolate frosting off the plastic wrap. "Maybe your dad's wrong," he suggested.

"You've got to be kidding!" said Rocky. "My dad is never wrong about anything."

29

"Says who?"

"Says . . ." Rocky hesitated. "Says my dad."

"Well, no one is right *all* the time," Daniel said.

"Says who?"

"Says *my* dad."

"Well, maybe *your* dad's wrong."

"Naw," said Daniel. "My dad's never wrong about anything." Daniel stopped talking and wrinkled his brow, thinking about what he'd just said. Then he started to laugh.

Rocky laughed too, but at the same time he felt mixed up, as though his birthday and his music exam fell on the same day. He didn't believe it was possible, but the thought of his father being wrong gave him hope. The thought of his father being wrong also made his stomach clench, as though a viola string had broken in the middle of his recital piece.

If his dad *were* wrong, perhaps Rocky could solve his problem after all. All he had to do was decide which his dad was wrong about—a man always having to stand up for himself, or never hitting a girl.

Just in case his dad was wrong about never hitting a girl, Rocky again raised his fist in Tink's direction. "Just you wait till after my recital," he shouted, "if you think you have a gap between your teeth now!" But Tink had started home and either couldn't hear or pretended not to.

But at least Daniel heard. "A-a-ll r-i-i-ght," he said. "Now we're cookin'."

It was the first time Rocky had ever threatened anyone. It made him feel better. Then it made him feel worse. What would Ferdinand or Martin Luther King think if they'd heard that? he wondered. Sheesh!

Just then a seventh grader came sauntering along the sidewalk. He looked at Rocky. "Hey, pwecious," he called.

"Oooos pwitty 'ipstick's smeared." Then he made fish lips and sent gross kissing noises in Rocky's direction.

"Terrific," said Rocky, rubbing the back of his hand across his mouth. "Just terrific."

"Orange lipstick and purple bubble gum." Daniel laughed. "You do look sweet."

Chapter Six

"So, what do you think?" Rocky asked. He was sitting cross-legged on the floor of Paula's bedroom, trying not to look at the posters on her walls. Those posters always distracted him and made him forget what he came to discuss, because they were all pictures of nearly naked women bodybuilders. There were pictures of women flexing their biceps and triceps and some other 'ceps Rocky blushed to even think about. Plus, the women all looked like they had been dipped in cooking oil, so they had this greasy shine that reminded Rocky of basted turkey breasts.

Paula had the posters because she wanted to be a bodybuilder and enter contests where you stood around rippling your stomach muscles while the audience cheered or hissed. If that was what Paula wanted, Rocky guessed it was all right with him. He just wished the poster women weren't so . . . so naked.

"What do I think?" asked Paula. "You mean about Dad always being right?" She stopped doing sit-ups and looked at Rocky. "Did you ever know him to be wrong about anything?"

Rocky closed his eyes so he could think better. "Yeah,"

he said finally. "He was wrong when he said I would never make a good viola player."

"So, that's once."

"And he was wrong about you too," Rocky continued.

"How so?"

"Mom told me he swore up and down before you were born, you were going to be a boy."

Paula's face turned so white, Rocky thought she was going to throw up right there on her carpet. "I didn't know that," she said, and the way her voice cracked made Rocky wish he had muzzled himself. "Well, I sure let him down on that score," she added. She tried to smile, but only half her mouth obeyed.

"*I'm* the one who let him down," Rocky said quickly. "I'm the one who plays the sissy instrument, the one who won't stand up for myself, won't punch out every jerk who crosses his eyes at me."

Paula brightened a bit. "Yeah," she said. "You're no prize either. Hey," she added, "looks like you've answered your own question. Dad *isn't* right all the time."

"So maybe he's wrong about a man always having to stand up for himself—or about not hitting a girl?" Rocky asked hopefully.

"Sorry. I think he's right about both of those."

"Thanks," said Rocky glumly. "Thanks a lot."

Back in his own room, Rocky took out a pad of yellow paper and sat down to make a list. Making lists always helped when he had to solve a problem.

When he was finished his list looked like this:

PROBLEM

How to get Tink O'Brien to quit using me for a punching bag.

SOLUTIONS

1. Monday afternoon, punch Tink right in the mouth.
2. Punch Tink right in the mouth *after* my recital next week.
3. Get someone else to punch Tink in the mouth.
4. Stay home sick every day.
5. Cut school for the rest of the year.
6. Do nothing and hope Tink will get tired of bashing me.

Rocky hoped to choose a solution that would help him stay peaceable, yet at the same time prove his father right about both defending himself and about not hitting a girl. He studied his list. Then he studied his list some more. Then he sighed. It was hopeless. Some solutions weren't peaceable at all, and every solution went against one or the other of his father's beliefs. With some, he didn't defend himself. With others, he hit a girl. and number 3—getting someone else to punch Tink—went against both of his father's beliefs. It was lucky, Rocky told himself, Paula hadn't bopped Tink. He took his pencil and drew a dark line through solution number 3.

"Dad can't be *wrong* about *both,*" he muttered to himself.

Once again Rocky studied his list, especially the first two solutions. Both those solutions meant Rocky had to punch Tink himself, either on Monday or right after the recital. They were definitely not peaceable. "Curses!" he said. He took his pencil and scribbled through the first two solutions, clenching the pencil so tightly his knuckles turned white. "Double, triple, quadruple curses!" he said. "No way!"

When he was finished, Rocky flung himself facedown on his bed, his head cradled in his arms. What a mess! All those solutions and none of them perfect. He didn't know what he was going to do. But one thing he did know: no way was he going to punch Tink O'Brien. Not on Monday, not after his recital, not ever. Not because he thought his father was wrong about standing up for himself or right about never hitting a girl. He wasn't going to punch Tink because the thought of hitting another human being—any human being—made him sick to him stomach. If that made him a chicken, he'd be happy to cluck!

Chapter Seven

"Hustle your buns!" Mr. Ryan sang out. "When I said I'd give you a ride, I didn't mean tomorrow."

"Coming," called Rocky. He grabbed his viola case and hurried to the car. I'm glad it's Saturday, he thought as he climbed in. All I have to think about is my music lesson. No Tink O'Brien bashing me around today. And after my lesson I'll decide once and for all what I'm going to do about her.

Rocky's dad sucked in a lungful of air, then cocked his ear toward his open car window. "Listen to that, will you. It's spring at last. Absolutely spring. Do you know what makes it absolutely spring?" He grinned at Rocky, who sat beside him.

Rocky felt something warm puddle up inside. That always happened when his dad was in a goofy mood. He grinned back, shook his head.

"The sound of dandelions popping up in the lawn." Mr. Ryan laughed and poked Rocky in the shoulder.

Rocky gave his dad a poke back, then reached up to tug gently at his dad's beard, something he had done ever since he was a tiny baby. "Toot, toot," he said. Then, out of the blue, he asked something he had been wondering about for ages and ages: "Why'd you name me Rock?"

Mr. Ryan chuckled. "Because Pebble didn't suit you."

"Come on, Dad. Seriously."

Rocky's dad chewed at his lip for a moment, then said, "It's a tough world. A kid needs a tough name to get through it. Rocky—Rock—is a tough name."

Rocky thought about that for a moment. He thought about the people he knew and tried to decide if they resembled their names. Daniel, for instance. His name reminded Rocky of Daniel in the lions' den. Rocky thought disobeying a king's command, especially when the punishment was being thrown into a den of lions, was a brave thing to do. He also thought it was a dumb thing to do.

His friend Daniel was like that. Rocky couldn't imagine anything braver than Daniel and his family sneaking out of Vietnam on a leaky boat full of frightened people. And then to come all across the world to America where they didn't know anyone, and according to Daniel's father, scarcely had a penny to spend or a pocket to put it in. That was brave.

But Daniel sometimes did dumb things too. Like the time he tried to trap a skunk that had taken up residence under his family's deck. Rocky hadn't gone near Daniel for a whole week after that. Trapping that skunk had been dumb.

Maybe people are like their names, Rocky thought. Some people. Other people. I'm nothing like my name. And neither is Tink O'Brien. Catherine. Not much wonder she has a nickname. Catherine sounds like someone you'd want to be friends with. Ha! Double ha!

Rocky tried to think of one other person with a suitable name. At last he said, "Paula's a tough girl's name."

"Yeah, it is," agreed his father. "And Paula's a tough girl. She'll do okay in this life." Mr. Ryan shook his head.

"I worry about you though," he confessed. "I wish I was driving you to football practice right now, instead of to a music lesson."

"Aw, Dad," said Rocky. The warm spot that had puddled up inside him evaporated. "You know I'm no good at sports."

Mr. Ryan sighed. Then he fingered his mustache and shrugged. "Oh, well. Paula makes up for your lack in that department. You're a good kid, even if you don't know a forward pass from a squeeze play. And you're a mean man with a viola—and a bowl of Jell-O." He chuckled and reached over to squeeze Rocky's shoulder.

That was the closest his father had ever come to telling Rocky it didn't matter that he was nothing like his name. Suddenly he wanted to lay his head on his father's wiry, black pillow of a beard, the way he had done years and years and years ago, when it was okay to be just a little boy who needed a hug. He wanted to tell his father about his problems with Tink. He wanted to say, Dad, you tell me I have to stand up for myself. But you also tell me I can't hit a girl. Now I'm in this corner. I can't stand up for myself without hitting a girl. And I don't want to hit a girl. I don't want to hit anyone. What can I do?

That's what he wanted to say. But he didn't say anything. For one thing, he didn't trust his voice. For another, his father's words had made him determined to do something to please him. He may have disappointed his father by playing the viola instead of football, but at least he could learn to stand on his own size six feet, to solve his own problems. He simply had to find a peaceable way to do it.

Too bad, Tink O'Brien, he said silently. You won't have Rocky to shove around much longer.

* * *

"Thanks, Dad," Rocky said when his father dropped him off a few minutes later. "I'll walk home."

Usually Rocky was Mr. Veraldi's first pupil, but today a strange woman sat silently in the waiting room and wonderful viola music swirled from under his teacher's closed door.

Rocky sat down to listen. Someday, he told himself, if he practiced a lot and didn't give up, someday he'd play that well—and make his father proud.

Just then the violist hit a sour note. The woman sitting across from Rocky grunted and drew her lips into a thin pink slash. When a second mistake screeched under the door, she began to scrape at her pink nail polish with sharp, angry jabs. With every jab, her black, spider-leg eyelashes twitched.

Watching the woman pick at the polish on her long, pointy nails, made Rocky think of his mother's hands with their rose-thorn scratches and chipped, ragged nails. He remembered her studying an ad for hand lotion, looking longingly at the model's fingernails.

"Someday," she had told Rocky. "Someday I'm going to have nails like that. When my ship comes in."

"What does a ship have to do with it?" Rocky had asked.

His mother had hugged him and said, "That just means when I get lucky and get rich." Then she had laughed a queer little laugh and said, "With my luck, when my ship comes in I'll be at the bus depot."

There were murmurs behind the door now and the sound of an instrument case snapping shut. Rocky looked up, hoping to see the student who played his instrument so well, but the woman leaped to her feet and stood in front of the studio door, her back to Rocky. So when the door opened, all he could see beyond the woman's green woolen cape was a pair of white leather sneakers.

"You made two mistakes, darling," the woman said. Even though she sounded pleasant, there was something nasty in the woman's voice that made Rocky's heart pound the way it did whenever his parents argued. Suddenly he didn't care who the musician was. Rocky just wished the woman and her kid were out of there.

Then Rocky saw Mr. Veraldi through the doorway. Running a wrinkled hand through his headful of startled white hair, he frowned and said firmly to the hidden student, "A good lesson today. You'll do well in the competition next week." Then he beckoned toward Rocky.

Oh, no, thought Rocky, as he got to his feet and hoisted his viola case. I hope that kid is in a different level. No way do I want to compete against him.

The woman turned and pushed past Rocky toward the door, leaving Rocky face-to-face with her kid. Face-to-face with Tink O'Brien.

Chapter Eight

Tink O'Brien! TINK O'BRIEN! Only she wasn't the Tink O'Brien Rocky was used to seeing, the one who lay in wait for him at Ambush Corner every day after school. There was no swagger, no daring in this Tink. This Tink stood with shoulders hunched, head pulled in, viola case hugged against her chest as though she were trying to hide behind it.

Even though she wasn't her usual swaggering self, the shock of seeing Tink riveted Rocky to the carpet. He stood, eyeball to eyeball with his enemy, his face flushing scarlet, his heart thudding. Each second that passed seemed like a thousand.

"Come on, Catherine. Don't stand there like an idiot. Let the boy past."

At the sound of the woman's voice, Tink's gaze darted away from Rocky and her shoulders twitched. Then she eased past him toward the outer door and was gone.

Rocky might as well have left with her. While Mr. Veraldi sat with lowered brows, Rocky screeched through his lesson, sounding as though he had studied music for four weeks instead of four years.

"Don't worry," his teacher told Rocky as he closed his viola case. "Some people believe that the poorer the dress rehearsal before a play, the better the performance. We'll pretend this was a dress rehearsal." He put a hand on Rocky's shoulder. "I'm sure you'll do well at the recital."

On the way home, Rocky's head was so busy gnawing at what he had learned that morning, he didn't notice the crocuses sprouting in the flower beds he passed. He didn't even keep an eye open for his favorite quail couple that lived in the area. That's how jumbled his thoughts were.

Then someone yelled, "Hey, Rocky!" and he had to think about something else and leave everything all jumbled up in his head.

Daniel pedaled up behind him on his bike. He braked to a stop, skidding sideways through a spring puddle toward Rocky.

"Hey, watch it!" Rocky yelled, jumping out of the way.

"Sorry," said Daniel, grinning and pushing his Giants baseball cap back on his head. "I guess you get knocked around enough without me doing it to you too." He swung off his bike and pushed it along beside Rocky. "Hey," he said after a minute, "what's with you? You look like you got bit on the butt by a bee." He laughed and started to chant. "Bit on the butt by a bee. Bit on the bee by a butt. Bee on the butt by—"

"What's with *you,* noodle nose?" Rocky interrupted. "You sound like you drank some loony juice."

"I'm just in a good mood is all," answered Daniel. "My dad told me this morning I can go to computer camp this summer after all."

Rocky groaned. "Camp. Don't even mention that word around me."

"Don't mention camp? Camp, as in go away to? Camp, as in have a lot of fun? Camp, as in learn new stuff? Camp, as in computer. Camp, as in *musique?*" Daniel was practically jigging around his bicycle by this time.

Rocky shifted his viola case to the other side and shoved his free hand deep into his jacket pocket. No gum. "You really have had some loony juice," he said glumly.

"Why don't you want me to mention camp?" Daniel asked. "All you talk about lately is winning that music competition next week so you can go to music camp. Well, I take that back. Camp's not all you talk about. Camp and Tink O'Brien."

"You cucumber!" yelled Rocky. "Don't mention either of those things. Especially in the same sentence. Oh, I think I'm going to barf!" He swung his viola up and wrapping his arms around the case, leaned his head against it.

"Hey, man," said Daniel, propping his bike against a handy tree in the Dickersons' front yard. "Don't strip your gears. At least not before you tell me what happened. Something did happen—*n'est-ce pas?*"

"Sort of," muttered Rocky into the side of his viola case.

"What do you mean, sort of?"

Rocky lowered the viola and shrugged. "Well, it's no big deal, really. Nothing that won't ruin my entire Saturday. Nothing that won't ruin the rest of my long, miserable life. Which probably won't be so long anyway—just miserable. No big deal."

"Spill it," ordered Daniel.

Rocky sighed, then lowered himself onto the Dickersons' front lawn. "Guess who I saw at my music lesson this morning?" he asked.

"How should I know?" said Daniel, scraping the toe of his sneaker through the grass, then bending down to study the results.

"Do you want to hear this or not?" asked Rocky. He

thought it might help to tell someone what he had learned that morning, and Daniel was a good listener.

Daniel plunked himself down beside Rocky, first making certain he sat on a dry spot of grass. "Shoot," he said.

"Tink O'Brien," said Rocky.

"What about Tink O'Brien?"

"That's who I saw at my music lesson this morning."

Daniel chewed on that bit of information for a second. "So?" he asked finally. "Did she punch you out in front of your teacher?"

Rocky shook his head. "Her mother was waiting for her. At least I think it was her mother. She had the same color hair. But she has these skinny eyes that look like they're going to shoot darts. And she talks in this syrupy voice that gave me goose bumps."

"At least she saved you from being a punching bag."

"Yeah, I guess I should be grateful for that."

"So what's the problem?"

"The problem is, Tink plays the viola."

"No-o-o-o w-a-a-a-y!" said Daniel.

"Oh, yeah," said Rocky. "And she's going to be in the competition next week."

"But that's perfect," said Daniel, drumming his legs up and down on the grass. "Skin her butt. Show her a thing or *deux*. Beat her where it really counts."

Rocky shook his head. "But she's good. Really good," he said. "So good Mr. Veraldi says she's a level above me already. So I won't be competing against her."

"Oh, crumb!" said Daniel, smacking a fist into a palm. "It would have been so perfect." He was quiet for a minute. "But if she's as good as you say," he continued, "maybe it's better that you aren't up against each other. It would have been really rotten if she beat you."

"Yeah, but it's really rotten anyway, 'cuz now I can win

and Tink can win—and you know what that means." Rocky groaned again and started ripping at the grass.

Daniel wrinkled his forehead and tugged at a hank of black hair sticking out from under his cap. "Oh, I get it," he said at last. Then he began to laugh.

"It's not funny," snapped Rocky.

"It is funny. Kind of," sputtered Daniel. "I just hope you have a nice time at camp. You—and Tink."

"I just hope I'm alive come fall," groaned Rocky. "But after a month at music camp with Tink O'Brien, I don't think it's possible." He flung himself backward on the lawn and crossed his arms over his face. "I think I'll throw the competition," he muttered.

"What do you mean?"

"I mean I better not win next Saturday."

"But that would be crazy! You've been dying to go to that camp. Listen, what you really need to do is fix this mess with Tink. I still say one good punch would do it, girl or no girl."

"You may be right," Rocky said. "One really, good, solid punch would end the whole thing. Tink would quit hitting me and I'd break my hand and be out of the competition. So no music camp with Tink. And even if I didn't break my hand, her big brother would simply pound me to death." He snapped his fingers. "Pffft! Just like that all Rocky Ryan's problems are over."

Only they wouldn't be over because Rocky wasn't going to hit Tink.

"Nope. I've got to try another way," said Rocky, pushing himself up. "And I think I know what I'm going to do."

"What?" asked Daniel. His dark eyes peered into Rocky's as though looking for the answer.

45

"I'm not going to give her a chance to hit me again." Rocky took a deep breath. "I'm going to ditch school."

"Ditch?" squealed Daniel. "How can you do that?"

"Easy." Rocky shrugged, acting much less worried about cutting school than he felt. "I'll just leave the house in the morning as usual and go home in the afternoon as usual. Only in between I won't be at school. I'll be somewhere else."

"Where?"

"Anywhere."

Daniel stuck a fingernail in his mouth and started to chew. "What if you get caught? Skipping's against the law, *n'est-ce pas?*"

"I'll be careful."

"But when you go home at your usual time, won't Tink be waiting at Ambush Corner anyway?"

Rocky started tossing the grass he had ripped out of the Dickersons' lawn from one hand to the other. "Not if she thinks I'm home sick. And maybe after a few days she'll get out of the habit of socking me. Or maybe she'll find someone else to knock around."

"I just hope it isn't me," said Daniel.

"I'll stay away a few days and then come back. If she starts in again, I'll cut again. But maybe she won't start again."

"Don't bet your viola on it," warned Daniel, starting to chew on a fresh fingernail.

"Why not?" asked Rocky. "If playing the viola means I have to go to camp with Tink O'Brien, I might never touch it again."

Chapter Nine

"Bye, Mom," Rocky said, and shut the door behind him as though it were another ordinary Monday morning. Only it wasn't. It was Ditch Day Number One.

I hope Daniel remembers to give Mrs. Crayton the note I forged saying I have strep throat, he thought as he headed down the driveway. I hope he remembers to meet me at Ling's store right after school to give me my homework.

A successful ditch, Rocky had learned, was a lot of hard work. You didn't just take off and expect to have a good time. You had to make plans. Making plans to ditch school, Rocky thought, was harder than going to school. But still easier than getting socked by Tink O'Brien.

As soon as he was out of sight of the house, Rocky changed directions. He didn't want to go anywhere near the school, so he headed toward the park four blocks the other way. He took long, purposeful strides, so anyone watching would think he had somewhere important to go. Even a turnip could tell Rocky was cutting school if he sauntered along checking out new leaves.

Rocky was about a half block from the park on a street he hadn't been down for ages, when the door of the next house opened and out walked Tink O'Brien. Rocky dodged behind a naked lilac bush as she turned to shut the door behind her.

Cripes! thought Rocky, praying she hadn't seen him. I did enough planning to give myself a very serious head-ache, only I didn't plan on this. He stood as still as he could, trying not to flicker a nostril, as Tink walked down the sidewalk toward him.

Please bush, grow some leaves, he begged silently as she got close enough for him to see the jagged zipper teeth of her open jacket. Close enough to see the row of tiny penguins strutting across the front of her pink sweatshirt.

It was then Rocky realized Tink wouldn't notice him even if he threw himself in the middle of the sidewalk. Because now she was close enough for him to see the tears flooding down her cheeks.

There were some things Rocky had decided he did not want to see in this world. A dying person was one of them. A bullfight was another. Now, to this list he added the sight of his worst enemy weeping. That surprised him, because he had expected Tink O'Brien in tears to be a wonderful sight, a moment of triumph. Instead, his stomach dropped, as though he'd gulped a load of gravel.

As she went past him, Tink made a couple of wet chok-ing noises and pulled the back of her hand across her eyes. Then she ran, her yellow backpack bouncing, her ponytails flipping.

When Tink had disappeared, Rocky edged out from be-hind his bush and toward the O'Brien house. He kept his head straight, but let his gaze slide over the house as he passed.

It was a lot classier house than his, with a gleaming brass mailbox and brass door handle. A stone lion sat at the en-trance. He tried to see in the window, but it was covered with those gauzy curtains that are never opened—the kind that always made Rocky feel as though he and the room were buried. What was the point of having windows, he wondered, if you couldn't see the sky and the trees and the flowers?

A few minutes later, Rocky was in Freedom Park. He kept going until he came out the other side onto a main street. Then he plunked himself down on a bench to wait for the next bus downtown. While he waited, he thought about Tink O'Brien.

Misery loves company, he said to himself. He'd heard his mother say that once when he'd asked her why she let that icky Mrs. Ghiardelli hang around so much. All Mrs. Ghiardelli did was whine and complain—about the clouds, about Mr. Ghiardelli, about her corns, about Mr. Ghiardelli, about the president, about Mr. Ghiardelli, about wax buildup, about Mr. Ghiardelli.

"Misery loves company," his mother had said with a laugh, "although why she picks me to complain to, I'll never know."

It hadn't made any sense to Rocky then, but now it did. Maybe Tink's miserable, so she can't stand to see anyone else happy, Rocky thought. Maybe that's why she's always picking on me.

Usually Rocky was a pretty happy kid. He loved his music. School was okay. He got along with most other kids and had one very best friend. His parents were human beings—most of the time. Even though they argued once in a while, they didn't pick their noses or scratch themselves in embarrassing places in front of his friends. Paula was kind of weird, but everyone he knew complained about a brother or a sister, so perhaps she wasn't as weird as he thought. Sure, everything around him wasn't *perfect*, but still, it all added up to an okay life. Except for Tink O'Brien.

Just because she's miserable doesn't give her the right to make me miserable, too, Rocky decided, as the bus belched to a stop in front of him. Ha! She probably knew I was behind the bush all the time and was trying to get me to feel sorry for her. Double ha! If she thinks that'll work, her chewing gum pack is short a stick.

Rocky got off the bus a few blocks from the downtown mall. Walking the rest of the way will help kill some time, he decided. Already he could tell it was going to be a long day. He felt as though he'd left the house years ago, but his watch told him the stores weren't even open yet. He reached into one pocket to make sure he had enough money for a movie, just in case the hours really dragged. Then he shoved his hand into the other pocket and found some gum. He popped a couple of sticks into his mouth and headed slowly down the street, but not so slowly it would seem he had nowhere to go.

About a block from the mall he ducked into a pocket park. It was a tiny green spot where an old building had been demolished. Between patches of grass were a few trees and some secluded benches. Rocky threw his backpack onto the bench in the farthest corner and sat down. This early, he was the only one there, so it was a perfect spot to fritter away some time. With a thick evergreen shrub at the street end of the bench, no one would see him unless the person came all the way to the back of the park.

A pigeon waddled across the concrete toward him, making coaxing noises deep in its throat. Rocky was glad to see it. He'd never spent time alone in a park before and the pigeon was company. He offered it a bite of the graham cracker his mother had put in his bag for recess. He was tempted to feed it his lemon yogurt, too, because he hated lemon yogurt, but he had a feeling pigeons wouldn't like it either.

The pigeon was pecking away hungrily when Rocky saw an old man saunter into the park, his eyeglasses glinting in the sunlight. He carried a polished cane that he swung in circles, now and then jabbing at a nearby bush. There was something familiar about the man's headful of startled white hair, hair that looked as though it belonged to a weird alien scientist who fooled around with electricity. Mr. Veraldi!

Rocky scrunched down behind the bush as the old man ambled on sneakered feet toward a sunlit bench. He held his breath until his music teacher had settled, his back to the street. Rocky was certain he hadn't been noticed. But now Rocky was trapped. He couldn't leave without going past Mr. Veraldi. He'd have to sit in the park until the old man left.

The pigeon nibbled around Rocky's sneaker, waiting for more treats. Afraid the bird would call attention to him, Rocky toed him away. Gurgling and cooing, the pigeon puttered through a spring puddle to Mr. Veraldi, its feet leaving twiggy, wet tracks.

Then someone else entered the park. A young woman this time. She didn't go straight to a bench, but strolled back and forth as though looking for someone. She didn't notice Rocky in the back corner.

The woman reminded Rocky of some of the women in Paula's posters. Her hands were in her jacket pockets, but her sleeves were pushed up and he could see knots and cords in her forearms. They reminded Rocky of the thick ropes he had once seen on a ferryboat. When she walked, her behind twitched. She had what his dad would call "a hitch in her gitalong." Rocky almost giggled out loud but stopped himself, remembering his mother's orders never to make fun of something a person couldn't help.

I bet she could help that if she wanted to, he decided, and nicknamed her Twitch Butt.

Seconds later, Rocky knew, really knew, for the first time in his life, what it was to be afraid.

Twitch Butt stopped, straddle-legged, in front of Mr. Veraldi. When the old man tried to rise, she shoved at him with an open palm, saying words that made Rocky feel as though a fist had been slammed into his stomach.

"I know you got it, Pops," she said. "I saw you at the teller machine. So why don't you just give it to me? Then I won't have to cut you."

Rocky saw a flash in the sunlight. A knife. Twitch Butt had a knife.

Chapter Ten

When Rocky saw Twitch Butt's knife, his first instinct was to run. But he couldn't get his muscles to move. He felt like Superman with a hunk of kryptonite in his pocket. He opened his mouth to yell, thinking Twitch Butt would scram if she knew she had a witness. But what would he yell? "Cut that out!"? When she had a knife? Real smart.

Cops! he thought then. I'll yell "COPS!" and maybe she'll think they're coming. Maybe one will even come.

He opened his mouth, but the sound that came out was no louder than a bird tweet.

Twitch Butt shoved Mr. Veraldi again, forcing him against the end of the bench. He reached an arm backward as though to steady himself, but Rocky saw his hand creep toward the cane he had hung on the bench back.

"Okay. Okay," he snapped, sounding braver than Rocky felt. "It's yours. Just step back. Let me get my balance."

Rocky held his breath. Twitch Butt cackle-laughed, stepped back one step. The knife blade glittered in the sunlight.

Mr. Veraldi's hand was on his cane. Suddenly he flung

himself to the side. His arm swung wide and the cane smacked across Twitch Butt's head with a loud thunk.

Twitch Butt staggered, shook her head. "You old hair bag!" she snarled. She took a step toward Mr. Veraldi.

A jolt like lightning zapped through Rocky, shoving him off the bench and onto his feet. Oh, no! he thought. I'm going to see another thing I never wanted to see. I'm going to see a dying man. Rocky knew, just knew Twitch Butt was going to knife Mr. Veraldi for smacking her like that.

But then, so fast Rocky saw only a blur, Mr. Veraldi brought his cane down on Twitch Butt's arm. The knife clattered across the concrete and skittered under a pine tree. Then the old man began twirling the cane in front of him like a baton or like those nunchaku karate experts use.

Twitch Butt was now facing Rocky, so he saw her eyes squint, as if she didn't believe what she saw. She took one step backward. Another. Then she stopped and glanced toward her knife. But when Mr. Veraldi took a step toward her, his cane still a whirling blur, Twitch Butt darted around him and started to run. In seconds, she had twitched out of sight.

When Twitch Butt was gone, Rocky realized he had been holding his breath. He let it out, took a gigantic gulp of air and held that before letting it out a dribble at a time. After three gulps and dribbles, his heart stopped flopping and his knees felt stronger. He noticed his gum was gone, no doubt swallowed.

Without even stopping to think of the consequences, he left his bench and hurried over to Mr. Veraldi, who was tucking in his shirt and tugging his jacket into place. "Are you okay, Mr. Veraldi?" he asked.

His music teacher straightened his glasses and leveled watery blue eyes at Rocky. Then, like a marionette whose strings had suddenly broken, he sank onto the bench.

54

"Rocky?" Mr. Veraldi gave his head a small shake, as though to clear his vision. "I'm fine. Fine," he said, puffing a little. "That wasn't the nicest way to start my morning, but I really . . . am . . . fine." He shook his head again, his hair bobbling. "This used to be such a nice city." He puffed a few more times, took one deep breath, the same way Rocky had just done, then expelled it with flapping lips.

"What can I do?" asked Rocky, leaning forward to peer into Mr. Veraldi's face. "Should I call an ambulance? A policeman! Do you want me to call a policeman? Here, let me help you up. No, stay where you are." Rocky knew he was babbling, but he couldn't get his mouth under control. He'd read about people going into shock and doing strange things after something traumatic happened to them. Perhaps he was in shock. Ridiculous, he decided. Mr. Veraldi, not he, should be in shock. Yet he couldn't stop chattering.

At last, the sight of a policeman hustling into the park stopped his tongue.

"Everything okay here?" the policeman asked, his hand on his nightstick. "We just saw a known perp leaving the park in a big hurry." He leaned over and hucked a gob of spit into a bush. "Anything happen we should know about?" The officer had a single eyebrow that joined over his nose, and now it rose in one lone, crooked, commanding line.

Mr. Veraldi nodded. "As a matter of fact," he said, "I was accosted by a young woman who wished to part me from my money. She had a knife." He pointed with his cane to where the knife lay under the pine. "Fortunately, she'll have to look elsewhere for her funds."

"He bashed her with his cane," blurted Rocky. Now that it was really, truly over, and he and Mr. Veraldi were okay,

55

Rocky realized the attempted robbery had been the most terrifying but also the most exciting thing he had ever seen. His excitement made him forget he didn't want to call attention to himself. As soon as he spoke, he wanted to disintegrate. Dumb, he told himself. Dumb, dumb, dumb. No doubt he'd be bounced back to school faster than Mr. Veraldi could say "Adagio! Adagio!"

The officer looked at Rocky. His eyes narrowed into crinkles under his single eyebrow. "You with him?" he asked Rocky, nodding toward Mr. Veraldi, his thumb circling the top of his nightstick.

Rocky could have sworn his tongue started to swell. For certain the blood fled from his head, only to come rushing back to pound against his temples, flooding all thoughts from his brain. "I . . . er . . . I . . ." he began, but couldn't go any further.

Mr. Veraldi stood up and laid a hand on Rocky's shoulder. "I'm Giancarlo Veraldi, professor of music. This boy is Rocky Ryan, my student."

The officer looked like he might say something else, and Rocky held his breath. "Gina Veraldi's father?" was all he asked.

Mr. Veraldi nodded.

"It's clear where she got her spunk," the policeman said. "Do you want to file a complaint, sir?"

"Of course," said Mr. Veraldi.

"You'll have to come to the station to sign it."

"Give me some time to recover first, then I'll come down," said Mr. Veraldi.

After the policeman agreed and left, Mr. Veraldi peered at Rocky over the top of his glasses. "You going anywhere in particular?"

Rocky shook his head.

"I thought as much. Care to get a piece of pie with me?"

Rocky nodded, not certain what else he could do. Oh, boy, he thought as he followed Mr. Veraldi out of the park and toward a nearby pastry shop, I'm in for it now.

Chapter Eleven

Rocky squirmed under Mr. Veraldi's stern gaze while they waited for their pie. He took a long drink of milk, thinking how he'd known his music teacher for four years, but didn't really know him at all. All Rocky knew was that Mr. Veraldi could play any string instrument invented and he had a daughter named Jean or Jen or something. And he'd learned about the daughter only a few minutes before, from the policeman.

Rocky suddenly wished he knew a lot more about Mr. Veraldi, especially what he might do about Rocky not being in school. So far he hadn't said a word about that, had just studied Rocky with those pale blue eyes of his.

It was those eyes, magnified by Mr. Veraldi's eyeglasses, that were making Rocky squirm. And the silence. Between the stares and the silence, Rocky was so miserable he didn't think he'd be able to swallow his pie when it came. At last he couldn't stand it any longer. He started to talk. "I'm sorry I wasn't any help. Back there. In the park. I was just so . . . so . . . scared, I couldn't do anything. I tried to yell for help. But all I did was . . . tweet. But I guess you didn't need my help anyway. I've never seen anyone twirl a cane like that. Anyway, I'm sorry. And I'm glad you're okay.''

Silence.

''Are you going to tell my parents?'' he blurted finally. Then he sat holding his breath while Mr. Veraldi took one, two sips of coffee.

''Tell them what?''

The breath he had been holding spurted out of Rocky with a whoosh. Did Mr. Veraldi not realize he was cutting school? Or was he toying with him? Better not take a chance.

''Tell them about me, you know, not being in school today?''

Rocky could tell from the look in Mr. Veraldi's eyes that he *had* known he was skipping school. He'd been waiting for Rocky to confirm it.

''Since I care about you, yes, I normally would mention it to your parents,'' the old man said. ''But knowing you, I'm sure there's a perfectly logical reason for you to be missing school. I do wish, however, that if you're going to play hooky, you'd spend your free time doing something worthwhile—such as practicing your viola.''

Rocky flushed with relief. He was safe. Suddenly he noticed how wonderful the pastry shop smelled. His stomach rumbled in agreement and he wished the waitress would bring his slice of chocolate mousse pie with whipped cream.

''I appreciate your concern for my safety though,'' Mr. Veraldi continued. ''And I'm glad you didn't get involved in my predicament. I would have been very sorry had something happened to you.''

Finally. The waitress plopped down the plates and went to get more coffee for Mr. Veraldi.

First Rocky ate a giant glob of whipped cream, swirling it around with his tongue and letting it slide down his throat.

59

Then he started on the good part, thinking "mousse" was a silly name for something that tasted so delicious.

While he ate, he watched Mr. Veraldi work on his piece of Dutch apple. The backs of the old man's hands reminded Rocky of a road map. Swollen blue veins for freeways. Crisscrossing wrinkles for side roads. Brown spots for cities and towns. Grandpa hands. But especially, Rocky told himself, musical hands.

Then Mr. Veraldi reached one hand toward the green tissue paper lying at the edge of the table. The paper was wrapped around two roses Mr. Veraldi had bought from a street florist on the way to the pastry shop. He absentmindedly rubbed the paper between his fingers, almost as though he had forgotten Rocky was sitting across from him.

I wonder who they're for? Rocky thought, raising his eyes from Mr. Veraldi's hands to his face, as if hoping to find a clue plastered there. Maybe he has a girlfriend. He almost laughed at the thought. Naw. Old men don't have girlfriends. They're probably for his wife—if he has a wife.

As though suddenly remembering he wasn't alone, the old man gave his head a little shake. He met Rocky eye to eye, then, as if he'd heard Rocky's thoughts, said, "Every week I buy one yellow rose and one pink rose. The pink is for my wife's grave. The yellow is for my daughter's."

Rocky's pie suddenly tasted like a lump of charcoal. "You mean . . . ?" He swallowed, a dry, gritty swallow that scraped his throat. Except for a great-uncle, he'd never known anyone whose wife had died. And he'd never, ever known anyone whose kid had died. He squirmed against the white wicker chair seat, not knowing what to say.

"My wife died twelve years ago," Mr. Veraldi went on in a normal voice. "I miss her, but it doesn't hurt so much anymore.

"Ah, but Gina . . ." He paused for a moment, then

continued, his voice ragged. "That was my daughter's name. That was only four years ago." He stabbed his fork into his pie and pushed it aside.

Rocky winced as though the man had stabbed him. But then, his curiosity aroused, he asked, "What . . . ? How . . . ?" but was unable to finish.

"She was a policewoman," Mr. Veraldi explained. "She was shot trying to make an arrest."

"Oh, wow!" Rocky heard someone say, then realized he had said it. "That . . . that's . . ."

Mr. Veraldi's face folded up on itself. "I know," he said.

Rocky decided that, yes, Mr. Veraldi did know what he was feeling. And suddenly he was comfortable with the old man again.

Then a tear dribbled out of the corner of Mr. Veraldi's right eye. He reached up with his napkin and dabbed at it.

Rocky's jaw dropped. Never, but never had he seen a man cry. "Men don't cry," his father always told him. Once in a while, when he was alone in his room, Rocky cried. But that was okay. He was still a boy. But he'd always known that when he got to be a man, whenever that was, he wouldn't be able to cry anymore, alone in his room or not. And now here was Mr. Veraldi wiping at tears like they were nothing. And in public too. Rocky shut his mouth with a snap of teeth. He blinked.

Mr. Veraldi must have noticed the surprised look on Rocky's face. His eyebrows bobbed above his eyeglasses and he shrugged. " 'What's gone and what's past help should be past grief,' " he quoted, before adding, "William Shakespeare. *The Winter's Tale.*" Then he snorted a harsh snort and thumped himself on the chest. "Not for Giancarlo Veraldi. I prefer his line from *King Henry VI:* 'To weep is to make less the depth of grief.'

"Don't ever be afraid to cry," he added sternly, his

61

piercing eyes narrowing and looking straight into Rocky's. "If women can be killed fighting for law and order, men can cry."

Rocky wasn't certain about that. One thing he was certain of: his father would never approve of a man in tears.

But then his father didn't approve of a lot of things—like a son who played a viola instead of football, a son who didn't like to fight. It was then Rocky realized Mr. Veraldi had done something else his father wouldn't approve of. Not only had he cried, but . . . Rocky couldn't believe he hadn't realized before now what Mr. Veraldi had done. Not only had he cried, but Mr. Veraldi had also *hit a woman*.

Chapter Twelve

Wow! Rocky thought. Mr. Veraldi did. He really did. He hit a woman. Double wow!

"So you think it's okay for a girl—I mean a woman—to be a policeman—I mean a policewoman?" he asked Mr. Veraldi.

"Why not?"

"But what about . . . ?" Rocky began. "Is it okay to . . . ? I mean . . ." He struggled to get the words out. "My dad says never to hit a woman," he blurted finally.

Mr. Veraldi leaned back in his chair. "Ah ha," he said. "And I hit a woman. Not a very nice woman, but still, a woman."

Rocky nodded.

"And what do you think?" Mr. Veraldi picked up the bill and studied it, waiting for Rocky's answer.

Rocky sighed. "I don't know," he said. "Maybe my dad's right." He dug around in his pocket and pulled out some money to pay for his pie and glass of milk. "But what if the girl's a bully, like that one who picked on you? Do you just let her be a bully because she's a girl? Or do you sock her a good one, like you did?"

"An interesting dilemma," said Mr. Veraldi. "Would it help you to know that most bullies have very little self-esteem?"

"Self-esteem?" asked Rocky, laying three dollars on the table.

"They don't think very highly of themselves. Perhaps they even think they're worthless, that no one cares about them. Sometimes—not always, but sometimes—a person will stop being a bully once he begins to feel better about himself—or herself."

Mr. Veraldi pushed the money back across the blue and white checkered cloth toward Rocky. "My treat," he said.

Rocky thought for a minute. "Whacking that bully across the head with your cane wouldn't make her feel better about herself, would it?"

Mr. Veraldi chuckled. "Hardly. Unfortunately, I didn't have much choice. Had I not defended myself, I might have lost my money—or worse," he said, pushing himself to his feet, slipping into his jacket and grabbing his cane.

Rocky thanked him for the pie, then followed, still jabbering. It was the first time he had talked about this to a grown-up, and it seemed his tongue had been waiting for a time such as this, because it flapped on and on as though he had no control over it at all.

At last Mr. Veraldi squeezed in a question. "It seems you've been doing a lot of thinking about this," he said. "Has something happened to set you off?" By this time they were outside the pastry shop and headed toward the police station four blocks away. Mr. Veraldi cradled the roses in one arm and swung his cane in the other, as though to keep in practice.

Rocky nodded. "A girl socks me every day on the way home from school."

"Hmmm-m-m-m. So that's why you're playing hooky. So you won't have to face this girl. An older girl is she?"

"No. She's in my room at school."

"And you don't want to hit her back?"

"No. Even if I did want to, I wouldn't, 'cuz I'm trying to be a peaceable person. Besides, I . . . I wouldn't want to hurt my hand."

"Excellent reasoning," said Mr. Veraldi.

"But that's what I can't figure out," said Rocky. "If I'm so worried about *my* hands, why isn't she?"

"Why should she be worried? Is she a gymnast, an artist?"

Rocky suddenly felt like he had run a mile. Sweat trickled down his sides and he was breathless. When he'd started talking about Tink, he'd forgotten she was Mr. Veraldi's pupil. Now he didn't know how much to tell. Should he name names? He wriggled out of his jacket, tried to think. At last he decided.

"She's not a gymnast or an artist. She's a violist, just like me. She's Tink—Catherine—O'Brien."

Mr. Veraldi stopped. He turned toward Rocky. "Catherine O'Brien? Catherine O'Brien is the bully you've been talking about?" He shook his head, looking as surprised as if a pigeon had landed on his shoulder and cooed a word into his ear.

"That's another thing I don't understand," Rocky said. "If what you say about bullies feeling lousy about themselves is true, why is Tink—Catherine—being a bully? She's a good violist, really good. She gets good marks in school. She lives in a super house. Sheesh, she should feel great about herself."

"She is an excellent violist," agreed Mr. Veraldi. "Very talented. But I'm not certain playing the viola was as much Catherine's idea as her parents'."

65

"But if she doesn't enjoy playing, how did she get so good? If I didn't like the viola, I'd never, ever practice. And I'd be lousy."

Mr. Veraldi started walking again, slower this time, as though he were thinking. "I don't know if I should be telling you even this much," he said, "but I'll do it simply because it might help you settle your differences with Catherine—and perhaps help you understand her." He paused, searching for words. "I suspect Catherine plays as well as she does and also excels in school because her parents haven't given her permission to fail."

Rocky hefted his backpack higher onto his shoulder. He thought of Tink's mother and how she immediately mentioned the two mistakes Tink had made during her lesson. He thought of how Tink had taken twice as long as the rest of the class on their math assignment, even though she knew all the answers, how she had looked kind of sick when she made one tiny mistake on a spelling test.

"You mean whatever she does has to be perfect? She can't make any mistakes?"

"That's what I believe, yes," said his teacher.

"My mother says we're supposed to make mistakes. Making mistakes is the way we learn."

"You have a very wise mother," said Mr. Veraldi, shifting the roses so he could give Rocky's shoulder a squeeze. "Perhaps we should introduce her to Mrs. O'Brien," he added with a smile.

"But now," he continued, as he resumed walking, "if you want to end Catherine's bullying, you have a decision to make. Life is a chain of decisions. Making the correct ones is never easy."

"That's for sure," agreed Rocky.

"But if we didn't make difficult decisions, right or wrong," said Mr. Veraldi, "we wouldn't learn anything worth knowing. So even though you may be hoping I'll offer you a solution to your problem with Catherine, I won't. You wouldn't learn anything if I told you what to do.''

Rocky's mouth curled downward in disappointment. He had hoped Mr. Veraldi was going to help him make his decision, but now it seemed he was merely going to spout theories. Phooey!

''But how do you know the choice you make is the right one?'' Rocky asked.

''Sometimes you don't,'' Mr. Veraldi said. ''I will say this though: often the right path is the one that may be hardest for you to follow. But the hard path is also the one that will make you grow as a human being.''

Mr. Veraldi stopped in the middle of the sidewalk. The gray granite of the police station was only a half block away. He pointed to it with his cane. ''And now,'' he said, ''I have to go and see a man about a mugger. Or, since she was a woman, is it a muggess?'' He chuckled. ''Good luck with Catherine. I'll be interested to know what path you take.'' He touched the handle of his cane to his forehead in a brief salute. He was nearly at the station when he turned back to Rocky and called, ''Now go home and practice!''

Rocky checked his watch. Barely eleven o'clock. If only I could, he thought.

Rocky spent the next few hours wandering around the mall. He wanted to go to a movie, but the only ones showing were what he called bash and blood movies, where the good guys bashed and bloodied the bad guys. Between Tink O'Brien and Twitch Butt, I've had enough bashing in my life already, Rocky told himself.

Doing nothing gave Rocky a lot of time to think, and for once that's exactly what he did. He thought about his father. He thought about Mr. Veraldi and what he had told him.

67

He thought about Twitch Butt. He thought about Tink O'Brien. He thought about his viola. He thought about music camp. He thought about Ferdinand the bull. He thought about Martin Luther King, Jr.

A bus heaved itself to a halt near the mall doors and Rocky ran toward it. Before this bus gets to my stop, I'm going to know what to do, he decided, as he leaped up the steps and flung himself onto a seat. He'd done enough thinking. It was time to make a decision.

Halfway to his stop, Rocky made it. Dad's right, he told himself. Sometimes you have to stand up for yourself. If standing up for yourself means hitting someone, then that's what I'll have to do—the same as Mr. Veraldi did with Twitch Butt. And if you do have to hit someone, it really doesn't matter whether the person you hit is a boy or a girl. Not today it doesn't. Dad's wrong about that. Besides, he told himself, if someone doesn't teach that Tink O'Brien she can't go around bashing people, she just might end up being another Twitch Butt.

His decision made, Rocky slouched down in his seat, expecting to feel extremely satisfied with his accomplishment, like a monarch butterfly that had just crawled out of its papery chrysalis and was waving its moist wings in preparation to fly. Instead, he felt as empty as the chrysalis the butterfly had left dangling behind.

"The right path may be the one hardest for you to follow," Mr. Veraldi had said. Had he made the right choice? Rocky wondered. Which would be harder: to go against his beliefs and plow Tink a good one, or to stand by his beliefs, stay peaceable, and go on getting socked?

Rocky groaned. Both choices stank. Both paths were difficult. "Help me, Ferdinand," he said under his breath, wondering what the bull would have done in a similar situation.

Suddenly Rocky sat bolt upright on his seat. He knew exactly what Ferdinand would have done. He would have done the same thing Rocky had been doing for the past few weeks. Nothing. Absolutely nothing.

"Why you silly old hunk of beef," Rocky muttered to his imaginary bull. "When things get tough, you just stand around smelling the flowers. Or worse, you sit down—or even lie down. I thought you were like Martin Luther King, Jr., but you're not. *He* knew when he had to *do* something. You don't *do* anything! You're . . . you're *wimpy!*"

It was then Rocky knew, truly knew what path to take. "Sorry, Ferdinand," he muttered, as he reached up to pull the bell for his stop, "but I'm not going to be a wimp like you any longer. You'll still be my favorite storybook character, but from now on you're not my hero."

He bounced down the bus steps feeling, no longer as empty, but simply as light as the butterfly chrysalis. "From now on," he said, loudly enough that an elderly man with a hearing aid turned to look at him, "from now on, it's just me and Martin."

Chapter Thirteen

As Rocky trotted back through Freedom Park, he noticed, as if for the first time, the swollen leaf buds, the twittering finches, the thick odor of spring-damp earth. He felt that, like the monarch butterfly, he really had been wrapped in a gray chrysalis for the past few weeks and had at last burst free. Feeling like this must mean I've made the right decision, Rocky told himself.

When he reached Tink's street, Rocky hid behind a spruce tree at the end of the block until he saw Tink go into her house and shut the door. Then he hustled past the house and toward his meeting place with Daniel.

Daniel was waiting at Ling's store, as promised. "Well?" he asked, hopping up and down on one foot. "Did you have fun? Where'd you go? What'd you do?"

While Rocky stocked up on gum at Ling's, he told Daniel all about Mr. Veraldi and Twitch Butt. He even told him how he hadn't been able to do anything but tweet.

"She had a knife? And he smacked her? Wow!" exclaimed Daniel when he heard, his black cowlick jiggling out the back of his Dodgers cap like an angry rooster's tail.

70

Then he added in an envious voice, "Boy are you ever lucky. I wouldn't dare ditch like you did."

"Of course not," agreed Rocky. "You haven't missed a day yet."

"And even if I did ditch, nothing exciting would happen," Daniel said. "Nothing like you saw. A girl mugger. Wow! I bet she made Tink O'Brien look like a sissy."

"That's for sure," said Rocky.

The boys started walking slowly, a sudden spring breeze flapping their pant legs against their ankles. They went past the Bennetts' with their dead birch tree. Past the Weims' with their chain-link fenced front lawn and its yellow patches of dead grass. Past the Kowalskis', whose entire front yard had been turned into a parking lot for their sons' junky cars. Past the Danzigers', who were so fussy about their yard you wouldn't dare spit on their grass.

"I think Tink really missed you today," Daniel said, kicking at a sheet of newspaper that tumbled past. "She went around with her mouth all droopy looking, like someone was picking on *her* for a change."

"Hey, that reminds me," exclaimed Rocky. "I know where she lives. Tink. I saw her this morning—and again just now." He told Daniel about running into Tink that morning.

"Crying? Tink O'Brien was actually crying?" Daniel said. "Amazing." He had just finished a chocolate bar and was now licking the goo off each finger.

Rocky unwrapped a stick of gum, then folded it carefully into thirds. "I figured out what I'm going to do about her," he said, tossing the gum into the air and catching it in his mouth.

"*C'est bien!*" said Daniel. "Al-l-l-l ri-i-ight! So what is it? What are you going to do?"

71

"It's not what *I'm* going to do," said Rocky, "it's what *we're* going to do. You and me. Daniel and Rocky."

"You want me to hold her so you can punch her lights out," Daniel said, hopping up and down and jabbing the air. "Right?"

Rocky shoved Daniel in the shoulder. "Wrong, beetle breath."

"You're going to hold her so *I* can punch her lights out?"

Rocky shook his head. "Nope. Nothing that exciting. First of all, I'm not going to ditch school anymore. I can't if I want my plan to work."

"This better be good," said Daniel, shaking his head.

"It is. It is. Now, here's what we're going to do—starting tomorrow morning."

When Rocky finished his explanation, Daniel stared at him, his eyebrows raised like horizontal question marks. "I think your viola is missing a string," he said.

"No way." Rocky laughed. "I'm not nuts. Honest. I think it's worth a try."

Daniel shook his head. "Totally loony."

"Does this mean you're not going to help?" Rocky asked, booting a dead cigar butt into the gutter.

"Of course I'll help," said Daniel. "We're best friends, aren't we? Besides, it'll only be skin off *your* nose if it doesn't work. And skin off your chin. And skin off your eye. And skin off your butt. And skin—"

"Okay. Okay," groaned Rocky. "I get the picture. Besides, it'll work. I know it will. Because it *has* to. It just *has* to."

"There's Tink," said Daniel the next morning before the first bell. "Let's see you put this fantastic plan of yours into gear."

"I've got to think of something first," muttered Rocky,

72

looking toward Tink, who was standing near the doors, her backpack slung over one shoulder. Today her dark hair was in one braid, which hung nearly to the middle of her back—like a boa constrictor ready to coil around his neck and throttle him, thought Rocky.

"Go on!" urged Daniel, giving Rocky a shove in Tink's direction. "You can think of something on the way over there."

"All right. All right. Don't be so pushy. I'll go. But after that it's your turn."

"Sure," agreed Daniel. "I already know what I'm going to say."

Rocky spun back toward Daniel. "Then you go first. That'll give me time to think of something super brilliant."

"Get over there," ordered Daniel. He planted his sneaker on Rocky's backside and gave him a push in Tink's direction.

Rocky's knees were quivering like a plucked viola string as he started toward Tink. Come on, he scolded himself, she's never done anything to you at school. Don't be such a wimp.

Still, by the time he was within spitting distance, his mouth was so dry he couldn't have licked a postage stamp.

At last he stopped. Tink was only three feet away, hearing distance, but not punching distance. She looked at him with those blue eyes of hers, eyes the same blue as the violas his mother had planted.

"Uhhhrrr-hhhrr," Rocky gurgled, trying to get control of his tongue, which seemed to have curled up somewhere deep in his throat.

Tink scrunched her eyebrows at Rocky. "Pardon me?"

"I . . . I . . . I just wanted to say that . . . that . . . youreyeslooknicethatway. No! No! I mean your hair looks nice that way. It matches your eyes. Kinda?"

73

"What?" asked Tink, her eyebrows even more scrunched.

"Oh . . . oh. Nothing! Nothing!" Rocky turned and fled.

"A lot you know, peanut brain!" Tink shouted at his retreating back.

"That seems to have gone well," commented Daniel, when Rocky reached him. "A wonderful plan, this plan of yours."

"Kiss off!" said Rocky. "I'm not used to giving compliments to my enemies. My tongue wouldn't cooperate, that's all. I'll get better with practice."

"Maybe your tongue knows something you don't," suggested Daniel. "Do you still want me to try?"

"Of course," snapped Rocky. "I told you what Mr. Veraldi said, remember—that bullies have no self-esteem. So if we can somehow make Tink feel better about herself—"

"She'll quit pounding on you," Daniel finished for him. "Okay, here goes."

Rocky watched Daniel stroll over to Tink. He said something Rocky couldn't hear. Tink nodded and then did something she had never done for Rocky. She smiled! Not a real lip splitter, but still a smile, if you believed dictionary definitions.

Daniel sauntered back toward Rocky. He shrugged as if to say nothing to it.

"What'd you say to her?" asked Rocky.

"I told her I was having trouble with a question on the math assignment, and since she's so good at math, I wondered if she could help me with it. That's all."

"But you never have problems with math."

Daniel grinned. "You know that. And I know that. But Tink doesn't know that."

"Good thinking," said Rocky. "Okay, since you're so

great at this compliment stuff, you can do it all. Then it won't matter that my tongue won't work."

"No way, José," said Daniel. "This is your problem and your plan. You'll do your share or I quit."

"Oh, all right. I just hope I can think of something to say that doesn't make me sound like . . . like . . ."

"A peanut brain?" suggested Daniel, echoing Tink's words.

"Yeah. Right. A peanut brain."

The bell rang and the boys headed inside. "Don't worry," Daniel reassured Rocky as they entered the classroom. "You'll get better at it."

"I hope so," moaned Rocky. " 'Cuz if this plan doesn't work, I'm hamburger."

Chapter Fourteen

After art class Rocky decided to give Tink another compliment, just to see if worrying had improved his ability. "I . . . I like your pigs," he said to Tink as the students were tacking up their watercolors.

"They're roses," said Tink.

And that's the way it went the rest of the day. When Rocky decided to tell Tink her eyes reminded him of the flowers his mother had planted, he said, "Did anyone ever tell you you have eyes the color of a *vee*-o-la?"

"Yeah? And you have eyes the color of a slug," said Tink.

"*Vi*-ola. *Vi*-ola. The flower," muttered Rocky as he retreated.

Rocky tried again. "I like that sweatshirt you're wearing. Too bad you got that red paint splotch on it during art class."

"That paint splotch is supposed to be there," said Tink. I designed the shirt myself—at the Splotches store."

"One compliment," Rocky told Daniel at lunch. "That's all I ask. I just want to give her one compliment that doesn't come out sounding like a sneer."

"She's got a cute nose," offered Daniel. "Have you said anything about that yet?"

"No. I've insulted her painting, her eyes and her clothes. I haven't sneered at her nose yet."

"That's it then. Just smile and say these exact words: 'You have a real cute nose, Catherine.' Practice it once, to make sure you get it right."

"You have a real cute nose, T-T-T-Catherine," Rocky stuttered. "Catherine?" he asked. "Why should I call her Catherine?"

"It's more respectful," explained Daniel. "Don't you know anything?"

"Okay. Okay."

"Try it again," ordered Daniel.

"You have a real cute nose, Catherine. You have a real cute nose, Catherine. You have a real cute nose, Catherine. How's that?"

"I think you've got it," said Daniel as the bell rang. "If you blow it this time, there's no hope. No hope at all."

Rocky waited until the class was busy with science projects before he cautiously approached Tink again. "Shut up in there," he told his heart, giving his chest a thump. He stopped near the sink where Tink was filling a beaker with water.

Tink turned her head to look at him. Her nose wrinkled and her upper lip lifted into a slight curl. Then her eyes squeezed shut and her bottom jaw dropped.

Rocky took a slow, deep breath, so deep he could have filled an entire balloon with one blow. "You have a real . . . cute . . . "

"AH-AH-AH CHOOOOO!" Tink sneezed.

". . . nostril, Catherine," Rocky finished. He groaned as Tink's eyes flew open and she clapped one hand over her nose. He backed away. One step. Two steps. Three, four, five steps.

"Did anyone ever tell you you're rude?" Tink hissed, her hand still over her nose.

"Not lately," Rocky muttered, still backing away.

"Well, you just keep your rude eyeballs off my nose, Rocky Ryan, or I'll knock them out and use them for marbles."

"At least I didn't spray you with germs," Rocky said, wiping his cheek on his sleeve. "You're not exactly a perfect example of good manners yourself."

"Then how about you teaching me some manners?" Tink dropped her hand and smirked. Rocky was certain her teeth grew pointed as he watched. "Let's say after school, at the usual corner?" Tink turned back toward the sink as Mrs. Crayton shook her finger at them.

"Brother," groaned Rocky to Daniel when the final bell rang. "I don't think I'll ever get the hang of this compliment stuff. Every time *you* say something to Tink, she smiles and says thank you. Every time *I* say something she growls and snarls and I come out a big zero. Which is probably what I'll be after she gets finished with my lesson in good manners."

"You're trying too hard," said Daniel, holding the door open to let Rocky through.

"Of course I'm trying too hard. My nose is at stake here! And my cheekbones. And my jaw. I only wish all the gushy things you said today had done some good." He pointed halfway down the block. "Darn. No matter how I hurry to get out of this school, Tink always manages to beat me. For sure she'll be waiting at Ambush Corner."

She was. Daniel picked out Tink's yellow backpack while they were still a block away.

78

"Boy, I hope she's mellowed out," Rocky said.

"I doubt the chances of that are too great," warned Daniel. "It took ten years for Tink to get the way she is. I don't think we can turn her into a perfect person in just one day—even if we did make her feel better about herself."

"Even if *you* made her feel better about herself," said Rocky. "I probably made her feel like slug slime."

"So what's the rest of your plan?" Daniel asked. "I mean, if all this compliment stuff doesn't work as fast as you'd like it to? Are you going to knock her into next week?"

For a minute Rocky didn't know how to answer that. He knew what he was going to do and why he was going to do it—because it was the right decision for him. But he didn't know if he could tell Daniel. Daniel was his best friend and he should be able to tell his best friend anything, but he wasn't sure he could talk about it, even to his best friend. Especially to his best friend. What if Daniel didn't understand? Or worse, what if he sneered?

That's a chance I'll have to take, Rocky told himself. If Daniel doesn't like me because of what I believe, then he isn't really my friend anyway. But Rocky's heart was fluttering in his throat as he opened his mouth to speak.

"This is what I've decided," he said. "First, with your help, I'm going to try to make Tink feel better about herself. Second, if that doesn't work, I'm going to stay as far away from her as I can. Third, if I can't avoid her and she's still a bully, I'm going to keep letting her . . . keep letting her hit me."

"Ooooo-wheee!" exclaimed Daniel. "Why?"

"Because I'm trying to be a peaceable person."

The boys had come to a halt in the middle of the sidewalk, a half block from where Tink waited. "You mean like that guy, Gandhi, in India years and years ago?'' Daniel asked.

''I guess,'' said Rocky, who didn't know much about Gandhi, but decided right then he'd learn about him as soon as possible. Martin could probably use some company now that Ferdinand was history.

''It's going to be hard,'' said Daniel, shaking his head.

''I know. But I hate violence. It makes me sick to even see it—like Twitch Butt and Mr. Veraldi. So I know it'll make me sick to be violent. And if I honestly believe in being a peaceable person for the rest of my life, I better start acting like a peaceable person. Tink will be a good test. It *is* going to be hard, but I'm going to try.'' Rocky held his breath, waiting for Daniel's reply. When it came, his breath flew out of him in a whoosh.

''Good for you, man,'' Daniel said in a quiet voice.

''You mean, it's okay with you? You don't mind that I'm going to act like a wimp?''

''Mind? No way. I saw enough scary stuff when I was a little kid in Vietnam to make me swear off *football*. I hate violence too.''

''But what about . . . I mean . . . you're always telling me to sock Tink. Or you're offering to do it for me.''

''Aw, that.'' Daniel hung his head and kicked at a gum wrapper on the sidewalk. ''I thought that was the way American kids were supposed to act. I didn't want to be called a chicken from 'Nam.''

''Whew,'' sighed Rocky. ''Am I glad you said that. I was afraid to tell you I want to be peaceable. I thought you wouldn't want to be friends anymore.''

''Well, I guess you're stuck with me—*mon ami*,'' said Daniel.

''And you're stuck with me—friend,'' said Rocky. He

80

grinned and smacked his palm against Daniel's in a joyous high five.

"Now come on," ordered Daniel, grabbing Rocky by his backpack strap and dragging him along. "Let's go and find out if kind words tamed Bully O'Brien."

Chapter Fifteen

"I'm going to make the first move," Rocky said to Daniel when they reached the corner where Tink waited, tapping her foot and twirling her braid with one hand. "Then maybe I can wriggle out of this."

"Good Manners: Lesson Number One," he said loudly. "Greeting Another Person." He bowed from the waist, then said, "How do you do, Miss O'Brien? It's so nice to see you again."

Tink wrinkled her nose. "That's not the lesson I had in mind," she said, but Rocky could have sworn she had a giggle in her voice. A tiny ember of hope started to smolder. Then Tink added, "Lesson Number Two: Teaching Rude People to Keep Their Eyes Off Your Nostrils."

POW! So quickly Rocky couldn't have ducked if he'd wanted to, Tink's fist slammed into his left eye. And for the first time she really connected.

Later, Rocky could swear you see stars when you get bopped on the head hard enough. His stars were mostly red and blue. At the time, however, all he could think of was how much his eye hurt, and how stupid he felt lying in the middle of the sidewalk.

"Why did she have to go and do that?" Daniel asked, as he helped Rocky to his feet.

Rocky shook off his dizziness and tried to find Tink with his good eye. She was shouldering her backpack by the bus bench. "I hope you didn't hurt your hand," he croaked. "You're a fantastic violist."

At last. A real compliment. Too bad it had come so late.

Tink looked at him. "Who . . . ?" she started to ask, but that's as far as she got.

"If it isn't fiddle fingers," Paula's voice said somewhere behind Rocky's shoulder. "Still getting beat up by girls, eh?"

Rocky spun around to see his sister coming up the sidewalk. A boy the size of a refrigerator was walking with her. A real blob, thought Rocky.

"What do you think you're doing?" the Blob asked.

Rocky tried to think of a sensible reply, then realized the Blob wasn't looking at him. He was looking at Tink. And Tink was looking at the Blob. She didn't look happy to see him.

"I'm . . . I'm going home," she said. Then she turned and ran, her backpack flopping.

"Boy, that's some shiner," Paula said, tilting Rocky's head back and peering into his eye. "It's going to close up on you."

"Great," said Rocky. "Just great. Tomorrow it'll no doubt be my other eye."

"Maybe not," Paula said, running one hand through her short curls. "I think I might have an answer for you. She jabbed her thumb in the Blob's direction. "This is Parker." She paused. "Parker O'Brien."

Rocky heard Daniel groan beside him and he knew why. Tink's brother. The Blob was Tink's brother.

"Parker and I have life science class together," Paula

continued. "I told him about the problem you've been having with—"

"You told him??!! You told him about *my* problem?" shouted Rocky. "You weren't supposed to do that. That was supposed to be private."

Paula raised her palms toward him as though to fend off his anger. "Sorry. Sorry," she said. "I was trying to help. You don't have to be so . . . so . . ."

"Ungrateful," the Blob said. "I think the word you're searching for is ungrateful. Of course, 'traumatized' would do too, I suppose."

"Creep," Rocky heard Daniel mutter. It wasn't often that Rocky formed an instant opinion of someone he'd just met, but he agreed with Daniel on this one.

"Don't worry, little buddy," the Blob said. "I won't spread your secret around." He put one meaty arm around Rocky's shoulders and said into his ear. "I was a sixty-pound wimp once myself."

Rocky squirmed away from Parker's arm. "Whatever Paula asked you to do, just forget it," he said.

"No can do. I made a promise. I told Paula I'd get my snot-nosed little sister to quit beating up her baby brother. And I will. Now just you don't worry about it. Okay, kid?" He gave Rocky a playful tap on the shoulder and almost flattened him for the second time that day.

Alarm and relief wrestled around inside Rocky. No more bullying from Tink O'Brien. And he didn't have to do a thing to end it. It was almost like having a fairy godmother carry out his wishes. Rather, a fairy godfather.

"Yup, don't worry about a thing," said Parker. "I know just how to take care of my baby sister." He smiled a smile that made the back of Rocky's neck prickle.

Minutes later, as he and Daniel headed the rest of the

way home, Daniel echoed Rocky's thoughts. "Poor Tink," he said.

"Yeah," Rocky agreed, his stomach squirming in misery. "Poor Tink. What have I let her in for?"

Rocky was holding a plastic bag of ice on his eye when Paula came home. He shook the bag at his sister. "Thanks a lot," he said. "It was bad enough I was getting beat up, now you're going to get Tink beat up too. And by her own brother."

"I told Parker to talk to his sister," said Paula. "I didn't tell him to bash her."

"Did you see the look in that guy's eye?" asked Rocky. "That was the look of a basher, not a talker."

"Don't get all revved up about it. I'll talk to him again tomorrow and make sure he doesn't pull any tough stuff. What do you care anyway, as long as his sister quits hitting you?"

"I don't know," said Rocky. "I just do is all." It was true. Rocky did care what happened to Tink. The thought surprised him, almost made him blush. "I guess I want everyone to be peaceable," he told Paula, searching for a reason, "not just myself." He gently pressed the plastic bag against his eye again. "It's closing up," he said, "just like you said it would. How am I going to practice for the competition with only one eye?"

"Come on," said Paula. "I know something we can try. It won't make the swelling go down, but you should be able to see out of your eye enough to play."

Rocky followed her into the bathroom. When Paula was finished, a narrow strip of adhesive tape stretched from his eyelid to his forehead.

"It looks stupid," Rocky said.

"Don't complain. It's holding your eye open."

"Yeah, thanks—I guess."

"Come on," said Paula, "I'll make you an ice cream sundae."

"With chocolate?"

"With chocolate."

"What are you going to tell Dad about that eye?" Paula asked, as she poured chocolate syrup over the ice cream.

"What are *you* going to tell him?" Rocky asked.

"Me?" Paula opened her eyes wide and fluttered her stubby eyelashes. "Why, I'll tell him my widdo bruver got punched in the eye by a widdle goil."

"You better not." Rocky lowered his voice so he'd sound more threatening. "You owe me—for ratting to that Blob O'Brien in the first place. So you just better not." Then, for good measure, he added, "Remember the J-e-l-l—O."

"You rat!" said Paula. "I *knew* you dumped that on purpose." She shook her fist under Rocky's nose. "Just for that I should smack your other eye." She paused, as if actually considering this possibility. "Naw, I'll just eat your sundae." And she scraped Rocky's sundae in with hers and ate them both, just like that.

Chapter Sixteen

"**W**hat happened?" Mr. Ryan asked Rocky when he came home. Rocky's eye had turned a glorious shade of red, blue and purple, and was swollen so fat it felt like he had a tomato plastered in his eye socket. But at least his eyeball wasn't bloodshot, and with the lid taped open, he could still see.

"Maybe his bow slipped during practice," suggested Paula. "Or maybe he kneed himself in the eye during gym. Or maybe . . ."

Rocky shot her a warning look. "I got it trying out for the field hockey team at school today," he fibbed.

"Hey, that's great," said Mr. Ryan, slapping Rocky on the back. "About the team, I mean, not the eye. What do you want to bet—?"

"I didn't make the team," Rocky said quickly, before his father got his hopes up too high.

"You mean they picked the team after only one practice? What way is that to run things? Who's the coach? I think I'll pop over after school tomorrow for a man-to-man chat."

"Forget it, Dad," Rocky said, squirming. He wasn't used to telling lies. In fact, up until Tink Time, he was about as good at telling lies as he was at paying compliments. "I don't like the game anyway," he said, starting to yap from nerves. "You run all over the field chasing a stupid leather ball with a stupid curved stick and trying to knock it into a stupid net the size of a wastebasket. At least it seems that small when I aim at it. And I keep getting the stick between my feet and tripping on it. Then someone takes a shot on goal and the ball smacks me in the eye instead of going in the net. Just look at it. It's a real mess. I need this eye, Dad. I need it for my music."

"You're right, it's a mess," said Rocky's dad, peering at his son's eye, then touching it gently. "And you do need it for your music. But what about after the competition this weekend? Maybe you could try . . ."

Rocky shook his head, sorry to have disappointed his father again—and with a lie at that. "No way. I might join a team someday, but it won't be a field hockey team."

"I'll bet it won't be a boxing team either," taunted Paula with a smirk.

"If I do join a boxing team, you better learn how to do a three-minute mile," Rocky told her, but it was just talk. He was so relieved Paula hadn't ratted on him, he might even have considered kissing her—if he wasn't worried about getting something fatal like rabies.

"Come on, you guys," Rocky's mother called from the kitchen. "Quit hassling each other and get in here and eat your liver."

"Yech!" groaned the three Ryans in symphony. "Liver."

"Can I put mine on my eye instead?" Rocky asked, as they headed for the table.

"Well, you made it," Daniel told Rocky. "It's Friday morning and Tink hasn't treated you like bread dough since Tuesday."

"Bread dough?" asked Rocky.

"Yeah. You know, when you're making bread and the dough rises, you have to punch it down and let it rise again, *n'est-ce pas?* At least that's what my mother does."

Rocky laughed. "Maybe I am bread dough. Every time Tink punches me down, I get up again."

"Maybe you're full of yeast," suggested Daniel.

"Maybe," agreed Rocky. " 'Course there're reasons Tink only treated me like bread dough once this week. Monday, I skipped. Tuesday, bread dough day. Wednesday, her mother picked her up after school. Yesterday . . ." Rocky rubbed his hands together and chuckled. That was the best of all. That was my . . . my . . . what is that French word you use for something special?"

"Pièce de résistance."

"Yeah, my pissda resistance."

"Even I'll admit sneaking out of the room when Mrs. Crayton wasn't looking was pretty tricky," admitted Daniel.

"I was probably home before the bell rang," said Rocky, doing a heel-toe dance on the sidewalk.

Daniel cuffed him on the shoulder. "You were lucky Barfbag didn't catch you."

"It was worth the risk." The boys stopped at the corner across from the school until the crossing guard could wave them on.

"I think Mrs. Crayton knew you were gone though," whispered Daniel so the guard wouldn't hear. "She kept looking around the room like she was counting heads, and I heard her muttering to herself."

"We gave her such a bad time yesterday, she probably thought she'd given me permission to leave early," suggested Rocky, "only she couldn't remember doing it and it was driving her crazy." The two friends started across the street. "Darn. That means she'll act like an FBI agent today, with me on her Ten Most Wanted List. I'll have to come up with a new escape plan today if I want to get away before Tink."

"There's only one problem with avoiding Tink all the time," said Daniel. "You'll never find out if her brother smartened her up or if all the compliments we've been spreading around like honey have done any good."

"Yeah," said Rocky, slinging his backpack onto a bench next to the school and sprawling beside it. "I've been getting good at the compliment stuff too. Tink actually smiled at me twice. Once when I congratulated her on her book report and the other in music class when I told her she sings as good as Vestal."

"Vestal?"

"You know, the lead singer of the Skinks."

"Oh, I remember," commented Daniel. "You're just lucky she likes the Skinks.

"You know what you should do?" he continued, plopping down beside Rocky on the bench. "If Tink's mother doesn't pick her up today, you should let her get to the corner ahead of you. That's the only way you'll ever find out if your plan is working. You can't avoid her forever. So why not find out before we waste any more time—or compliments?"

"The competition is tomorrow and I wouldn't want to play with another fat eye. Maybe I should wait until Monday."

"Okay," said Daniel. "But you better come up with an excellent escape plan if *Madame* Crayton gives you the eagle eye today."

* * *

"So much for new escape plans," muttered Rocky after school, as he and Daniel headed home. "Nothing worked, not even telling Mrs. Crayton that Tink offered to stay late to clean the hamster's cage. I'll bet Tink is already at Ambush Corner."

"Okay, so listen to me," Daniel said, shaking a finger under Rocky's nose. "I know you're trying to be peaceable and all, but there's nothing that says a peaceable person has to just stand and take it."

"You mean it's okay for a peaceable person to act chicken and run away," said Rocky.

"No! That's not what I mean. Well, yes, it is. But it doesn't mean you're a chicken. It just means you're trying to . . . trying to—"

"Save my tail feathers," suggested Rocky. "I don't know. Sometimes I still feel bad that I won't fight back. But I don't think running away would make me feel any better. Besides, you told me yourself *you* didn't want to be called a chicken. And now you're telling me to cluck."

"Not cluck, exactly," said Daniel. "I was thinking more of flapping out of the way—quickly."

"I'll think about it. Anyway, who knows? Maybe she won't be there. Maybe she'll be there and will just want to talk. Maybe she'll be there and—"

"Give you a big, mushy kiss." Daniel smirked, dancing around Rocky. " 'Oh Rocky,' she'll say. 'I just love the way you give compliments. Give me another. Say something nice about my eyes again.' Smooch! Smooch! Smooch!"

Rocky shook his head. "Daniel Tuan, you're the biggest zit I know."

"But you like me anyway, *n'est-ce pas?*"

"Right," admitted Rocky. He never could get very ticked at Daniel.

* * *

Rocky wasn't surprised when Ambush Corner came into view and he saw Tink's yellow backpack lying on the bus bench. Then Rocky saw Tink and everything stopped for him. He forgot to breathe, to blink, to take a step, to close his mouth, now hanging open in shock. Beside him, Daniel gave a short gasp.

Tink wasn't alone at the corner. Her brother, the Blob, was there, and another kid Rocky didn't know. The two boys, standing about four feet apart, were shoving Tink back and forth between them.

"Relax," Parker said. "This is fun. Let's hear you laugh."

"Leave me alone," begged Tink, "or I'll tell Mother."

"So tell her. Do you think she gives a monkey's tail about you?" The Blob shoved her toward his friend. His friend shoved her back. Tink staggered toward her brother, lost her balance and tumbled to the pavement.

She was crying when Parker dragged her to her feet and sent her lurching toward his buddy.

Rocky stood, frozen. Watching. Just like with Twitch Butt. Watching.

Chapter Seventeen

Watching Tink and the two boys, Rocky felt only numbness, the same numbness as when he saw Twitch Butt threaten Mr. Veraldi. His spit dried up so fast his tongue stuck to the roof of his mouth. A sour taste oozed up the back of his throat and he thought he was going to throw up right there on the sidewalk.

Then suddenly he was running, shedding his backpack as he went. Tink was only a house away, so Rocky barely had time to get up his speed. Before he even thought about what he was doing, he leaped into the air and flung himself onto the Blob's back.

His landing knocked the breath right out of Rocky, but he clung to the Blob's jacket collar like a baby possum clings to its mother's fur.

From the corner of his eye, he saw Daniel hurl himself at the other bully and lock his arms around one of the older boy's legs. The boy shook his leg as though he had a rat up his pants and called Daniel some nasty names. After that, Rocky didn't notice any more.

The Blob had grunted when Rocky hit, and staggered a bit, but Rocky didn't seem to be having much effect on him. Effortlessly, Parker snorted and roared, twisted and turned, trying to pitch Rocky off his back. Even though Rocky was terrified, into his head flashed the picture in *Ferdinand* where the bull charged around after being stung by the bee. Then Rocky saw fingers the size of jumbo wieners clutching at him and remembered the Blob wasn't Ferdinand.

Bending over as far as he could, Tink's brother reached behind his head, grabbed Rocky around the neck, dragged him over his head and flung him onto the sidewalk. Rocky heard a faint crack as he landed on his back and knew it didn't matter anymore what Parker did to him, because he had obviously split his skull open and his brains had to be leaking all over the concrete. He only hoped Parker would slip in the mess and crack *his* head open, too.

The tree beside the bus bench looked tiny and far away, as though he were looking at it through the wrong end of a pair of binoculars. Then everything started to come back into focus and he saw Tink shoving at her brother. She seemed to be calling him names.

The Blob bent over Rocky and Rocky waved a feeble fist in the air, hoping he looked dangerous. But he didn't, because he had closed his eyes. Then he heard Tink say, "Leave him alone." There was a grunting noise and the shuffle of feet.

You bet I'll leave him alone, Rocky thought fuzzily, trying to get his tongue to work.

Then he was thinking perfectly clearly again. His eyes flew open and he sat up. He looked quickly behind him, but didn't see any bloody mess where his head had been. He hadn't cracked his skull open after all.

"Why should I leave him alone?" sneered Parker, giving Tink a shove on the shoulder. "What's he to you? Your boyfriend or something? Naw. You're too stupid and ugly to have a boyfriend.'' He turned to Rocky. "And you. You little creep. I try to do you a favor and get my brat sister off your back, and you jump me. If you weren't Paula's brother, I'd . . . I'd scramble your brains for breakfast.''

Rocky shoved himself to his feet. He drew back his shoulders and shoved out his chest. "Go ahead,'' he challenged, hands on hips. "Since you get your kicks knocking around people half your size, go ahead. Make yourself feel good. Do whatever floats your boat. Scramble my brains.'' Rocky's heart was thundering so loud he was certain the Blob could hear it. He crossed his fingers, hoping he wouldn't faint and make a total idiot of himself. Not now.

Parker looked at Rocky, his eyes narrowed to slits. Rocky forced himself to match him stare for stare. Parker curled one hand into a fist nearly the size of Rocky's head. He took a step toward Rocky.

"Man must overcome violence without resorting to violence,'' Rocky chanted softly to himself. "Man must overcome violence without—''

"Will you forget that little snot and get this leech off my leg, man,'' demanded the Blob's buddy at that moment, pointing to Daniel, who still clung to his leg like a famished bloodsucker.

Parker hesitated, looked at his friend, then at Rocky.

Rocky waved his hand, beckoning the Blob to battle. "Scramble my brains,'' he called, thinking his brains must already be scrambled from his head being cracked on the sidewalk, or he'd know enough to shut his yap. "Come on, scramble my brains, big brave bully.''

Parker took one more step in Rocky's direction, then stopped. "Aw, kiss off,'' he said, then turned and pried Daniel off his friend's leg.

"We did it, Martin,'' Rocky whispered as the two bullies stalked down the street, shaking their heads in disgust.

"WE DID IT!" Daniel shouted, leaping to his feet and bouncing up and down, boxing the air with his fists. "CLUCK! CLUCK! CL—UCK!" he yelled at their retreating backs. "CLUCK! CLUCK! CL—UCK!"

There was an awkward silence when Daniel finally stopped clucking. Rocky eyed Tink. Tink eyed Rocky. Daniel eyed Tink and Rocky.

At last Tink spoke. "How's your head?"

"Fine," Rocky fibbed, fingering the lump that had started to grow. "Paula thumping on it must have turned it to rock."

"Your big sister picks on you?"

"A bit," Rocky admitted. "Not anything like your brother though," he added quickly.

"He's usually not that bad."

Daniel went and sat on the bus bench and started examining his pant legs. "Holes," he moaned. "That turkey wore holes in my knees dragging me around on my stomach."

Tink and Rocky didn't pay him any attention. "You okay?" Rocky asked her, noticing her scraped knee.

Tink nodded. "Hey," she said then, looking right at him with her viola-colored eyes. "Thanks. For . . . for helping me out. You too, Daniel," she added.

Rocky could feel a flush creeping above his collar. It was the first time Tink had ever said something nice to him. And it was definitely the first time she had ever looked at him that he didn't imagine her eyes shooting spitballs. "That's okay," he said with a shrug. "Forget it."

"Yeah, forget the thanks," groaned Daniel. "What I need is a new pair of pants."

"I'll give you a pair of my brother's," joked Tink. "His favorite pair. It would serve him right."

"Yeah, great idea," said Daniel. "That way Rocky and

96

I could both wear them—at the same time." Daniel started to laugh. Then Tink joined him and Rocky realized he'd never heard her laugh before. Soon the thought of him and Daniel waddling around together in a pair of the Blob's pants set him off too. And the harder he laughed, the lighter he felt, as though he'd shed a load he'd been hauling around for a lifetime.

"While you're at it, why don't you throw in a couple of shirts," joked Daniel.

"And a jacket or two," added Tink.

"Don't forget the BVD's," said Daniel, bending over in a spasm of snickers.

"Forget the BVD's," said Rocky. He blushed again. How could Daniel even mention something as embarrassing as underwear in front of a girl?

"Yeah, on second thought, forget the BVD's," agreed Daniel.

Suddenly, they all stopped laughing. Tink bent over to examine her scraped knee. Daniel started poking at his torn pants. Rocky tugged at his shirt, twisted from his ride on Parker's back.

"You'd better get your backpack," Tink said to Rocky, when they were able to look at each other again without giggling or turning red.

As he walked back to get it, Rocky noticed he felt strange, different somehow. He thought it might be because he'd broken his pledge to be peaceable. But it wasn't that kind of feeling, not a gut-aching, regretful kind. It was a good feeling, but it was more than simply the lightness he had noticed when he had been laughing so hard. It was more like the proud feeling he got when he had performed well in a music exam or a recital. He'd done something he didn't think he'd ever do. He'd stood up to a bully. He'd made a difference. But he hadn't done it for himself. He'd done it for someone else. And for some reason that made it seem even more special. For some reason that made him feel even prouder.

Tink was still waiting when Rocky started back. Oh no! Rocky thought. What if she's waiting to pound me again? What if saving her skin didn't accomplish a thing?

There was only one way to find out, he decided, and walked right up to Tink.

"Daniel just told me you play the viola, too," Tink said, "and that you're in the competition tomorrow. When I saw you at Mr. Veraldi's, I didn't see your instrument."

Rocky nodded. "I'm a level behind you," he said quickly. "I'm glad, because you'd whip me. I heard you play at your lesson that day. You're really good."

Stupid! Rocky told himself. Why'd I have to go and say the word *whip?* I hope it doesn't remind her to sock me one.

Tink didn't say anything, but a tiny smile appeared at the corner of her mouth, and Rocky thought he was home safe. Then Daniel said, "Better to get beaten at music than beaten on the head, eh, Rocky? And beaten on the nose. And beaten on the mouth. And beaten on the eye."

"Thanks a lot," Rocky muttered, certain Daniel's remark would prod Tink into punching him.

Tink took a step toward him and Rocky knew, really knew, his Rocky-to-the-rescue act had been for nothing. His stomach folded into a clump. "Man must overcome violence . . ." Rocky whispered to himself.

Tink opened her mouth. Rocky waited for the nasty remark she usually made before socking him. ". . . without resorting to violence," he continued. "Man must overcome . . ." He closed his eyes.

"I'm sorry," Tink said.

98

Rocky opened his eyes, blinked. "Huh?" Her voice was so soft Rocky wasn't sure he'd heard right.

"I'm sorry." This time Tink said it louder and looked Rocky right in the eye. "For . . . you know . . . hitting you." She shrugged. "I don't even know why I did it."

Rocky's stomach unfolded and he felt warm from the top of his head to his toes. He felt so wonderful he almost wanted to give Tink a hug. Almost. "That's—that's okay," he managed to stutter.

Tink smiled and reached down to grab her backpack and sling it over her shoulder.

He was tempted to ask Tink if being sorry meant she wasn't going to hit him anymore, but before he could, she asked, "All those times I socked you, how come you never hit back, anyway?"

Rocky hadn't expected that. He dug around in his pants pocket for some gum while he decided how to answer. "My dad says I'm never supposed to hit a girl," he said finally. "Besides, I didn't want to wreck my hands before the competition."

"Oh," said Tink.

"Oh, get off it," snorted Daniel. "Why don't you just admit you didn't hit her because you're trying to be peaceable? There's nothing wrong with that, you know. She's not going to think you're a sissy or anything. Not after the way you went after her brother."

Tink jerked her head in Daniel's direction. "That true?"

Rocky sighed. He nodded.

"Oh," said Tink again, starting down the street. "I never met a pacifist before."

"A pacifist?" asked Rocky, certain a pacifist was some sort of weird, disgusting creature.

"Yeah, a pacifist—someone who doesn't like war or violence." Tink was far enough away she had to shout. Then she added the words that left Rocky wondering if he were going loony or if the day had merely been a day full of odd happenings. "That's neat."

Rocky looked at Daniel, his mouth hanging open.

Daniel grinned. "Yup, you heard right. She thinks it's neat." He rolled his eyes, pointed at Tink then at Rocky, and started making kissy lips.

Ignoring him, Rocky gathered his wits enough to call, "Good luck tomorrow."

Tink turned and walked backwards for a few steps. "You, too," she yelled.

As Tink disappeared around a corner, Rocky realized that, for the first time since she came to his school, the thought of seeing Tink O'Brien the next day didn't fill him with dread.

"Yeah, see you tomorrow—Catherine," he whispered.

Chapter Eighteen

Tink was playing . . . Rocky searched for just the right word for her performance. She was playing . . . magnificently, he decided at last.

Rocky was glad he had already finished his piece. Now he could relax. Before he'd performed, he'd been so nervous he hadn't heard a single note any other musician had played, so nervous he was absolutely positive his bow was going to squirt right out of his sweaty hand and conk someone in the front row. Then it had been his turn, and except for one wrong note, he had performed better than he had ever performed before—and he had won first place in his division. Now it was Tink's turn and he was feeling easy in his mind.

He sneaked a peek around him at the listening audience. At Tink's mother, holding her body rigid, winding her hands with their pointy red nails around and around and around each other. At Mr. Veraldi, his eyes closed, lost in the music, a quiet smile on his lips. At the adjudicator, the woman who decided who'd win, staring at Tink as though she could see the notes rising in the air above Tink's instrument.

There was loud applause when Tink finished, but Rocky

noticed Mrs. O'Brien did not clap, but sat with her eyes squeezed shut and her hands now clenched in her lap. The Blob, seated beside her, was clapping though, slow, lazy claps, as though he didn't want to use up any precious muscle power on his sister.

Rocky looked at *his* sister, sitting beside the Blob, and shook his head in wonder. "You're going to the competition with Parker O'Brien?" he remembered asking the night before, his voice rising to a squeak in disbelief. "That big blob of a bully? I think all that weight lifting has made you brain dead."

Paula had smiled. "My brain is just fine, thank you. You see," she continued in a whisper, "Parker has this fantastic set of weights at home he told me I could use any time I want."

"That's no reason to go on a *date* with him," Rocky had told her, narrowing his eyes. "Besides, it seems kind of . . . kind of cold-blooded—being nice to someone because you want to use his weights."

"Give me some credit, will ya?" Paula said, tugging Rocky's ear. "After you told me what happened this afternoon, I decided there's one thing Parker needs almost as badly as his sister does."

"What does he need?" asked Rocky. "What? Another baby sister to pound on?"

"A friend," Paula had replied quietly.

The applause for Tink ended, and as the next performer started, Paula looked over at Rocky and winked. He grinned back, proud of his burly big sister, even if she had ratted to his parents about his fight with Parker.

"You did *what?*" his mother had shouted in dismay the night before, when Paula told what he'd done.

"*You* did what?" his father had asked in disbelief. Then, while his mother anxiously examined his hands and the lump on the back of his head, his father's eyes had met his. "I'm proud of you, son," he said. "I guess it has finally sunk in that it's important to stand up for yourself in this world."

Rocky shook his head. "It's more important to stand up for someone who can't stand up for herself," he had answered.

His father looked startled, opened his mouth as though to speak. Then he, too, had shaken his head. He didn't say any more to Rocky about the fight, but while Rocky practiced that evening, he would look up to find his father studying him, a crease on the bridge of his nose and his eyebrows bunched, as though he were seeing, truly seeing his son for the first time.

A short time later, Tink's name was announced as the winner at her level of competition. Then the adjudicator called all the winners still in the audience up on stage.

Before Rocky stood up, his mother kissed him on the cheek. "I love you, Rocky," she said.

His father rose to let him pass. Then suddenly he wrapped his arms around Rocky and lifted him off the floor in a gigantic bear hug. "Congratulations, son," he whispered, before setting him down.

As Tink climbed the steps to join Rocky and the other winners onstage, Rocky wondered why she didn't smile. Then he noticed she was watching her mother in the audience. Her mother looked as serious as Tink. Then Mrs. O'Brien rose to her feet, her face divided wide with a smile. She kissed her fingers and blew the kiss toward her daughter. And suddenly Tink was smiling too.

But Tink looks more relieved than happy, thought Rocky. I guess she didn't think she'd done well until her mother told her she had. Mr. Veraldi must have been right for sure. Tink doesn't have her parents' permission to fail. Poor Tink.

Rocky leaned over and touched her on the shoulder. "See you in camp, Tink," he whispered.

Tink turned her eyes to him. Viola-colored eyes. Friendly eyes. She smiled. "Yeah," she whispered back. "See you in camp. And Rocky," she added. "My friends call me Catherine."

The adjudicator called for one last round of applause for all the winners. Rocky stood, proud and content, watching his mother blow *him* kisses, while his father, hooting like a crazy man, raised his arms over his head and shook his clenched hands together in triumph.